CANDACE

&

OTHER STORIES

by Alan Cheuse

Apple-wood Press   1980   Cambridge/Newton

Acknowledgments

The author would like to thank the editors of *The Black Warrior Review* in which "The Quest for Ambrose Bierce" previously appeared.

"Fishing for Coyotes" appeared originally in *The New Yorker*.

Candace & Other Stories © 1980 Alan Cheuse

ISBN: 0-918222-18-4 hardcover
ISBN: 0-918222-19-2 paperback

Some of the places and institutions mentioned in this book do exist. The people of the stories do not exist nor have they ever existed. They are not real. Any resemblance to persons living or dead is unintentional and coincidental.

CANDACE

&

OTHER STORIES
by Alan Cheuse

To Marjorie

Contents

The Call

The woman's voice separated her from the multitudes who communicated each day by means of the great city's telephone system. A deep, wheezing gasp, like the astonished outcry of a dying passenger on a voyage she had begun in good health, it seemed at first hearing to bestow a certain difference, if not distinction, upon my little quest.

"Who are you?"

Not the measured North American "hello" I was accustomed to or the terse, nearly always shouted *Buay-No?* which most natives of the city hurled into the mouthpiece on first picking up the receiver, her words caught me quite by surprise.

I backed up a bit in the mental spaces that separated us, me on the edge of my narrow bed in a dark hotel room in the center of the city, the woman at a location as yet unknown to me — I had a letter with a postal box only as a return address — though somewhere within the boundaries of the city's trunkline.

"Who are you? Do you know who I am?"

My mind flew three thousand miles north and east and then roared back again to the moment's problem. Had I been placing the call from my office I might have been less tense about how to handle the difficulty which seemed to be increasing at each word. One marriage and two children later, I had put the wreck of myself back together and had an assignment for a story that was going to change more than my life. Like a man favoring an injured limb, I began to speak in a quiet, what I took to be friendly, voice explaining as succinctly as possible the purpose of my call.

"That's not what you want."

Confused for a moment, I lay back on the rough coverlet of my single bed and repeated myself. Despite the temperate climate year round of this city more than a mile above the level of the sea, little sunlight penetrated the cloud cover. Factories to the north coughed out dark smoke, winds pushed the clouds south, mountains behind the city cradled the thickening yellowish air. My room was dim, desolate.

"I know who you are. We met last year."

"I don't think so. I've never been to—"

"You're here! My God, why didn't you say so? Listen, my husband's not home now. Are you downstairs? We can talk."

"I'm in my hotel now. But if you tell me—"

"But you're here. So we can talk. I need to explain to you some of the awful things that have been taking place here. May I tell you truthfully? Forty-five years have gone by without a word of truth. Are you downstairs? My husband will be home soon. We need to prepare ourselves for his arrival. Can we talk?"

"Certainly we can talk. But if you tell—"

"I wouldn't say that if I were you. It's perfectly possible to be truthful downstairs. But up here, I go to my room for such occasions. Didn't you see me leave last year when you came to see my husband? What point of view do you hold?"

"Point of view?" I pretended I didn't understand. But it seemed then the first thing she said that made any sense at all.

"Are you religious?"

"What?"

"Let me write that down. Please, hold the line. I need to find my glasses—" Her distinctive breathing faded from the wire, and just below the level of comprehension the twit and chatter of four or five other conversations settled like dust motes on my inner ear. I took out my pencil, doodled in my notebook. I would get my message through and arrange for a rendezvous later in the week. I could pretend with others that my purpose was ordinary, traditional. But a great deal more depended on it than I had cared to admit to anyone but myself.

"Are you political?"

Her voice jarred me into sitting up on the edge of the bed. My pencil fell from my grasp and rolled under the night table.

"Are you downstairs?"

I banged my shoulder retrieving the pencil and suppressed a moan of pain.

"May I give you—"

"Sometimes my husband curses God. He says that God is not listening to us. This of course goes to the heart of the system. Forty-five years I have been his companion and now he wants to go travelling with another woman. You're young. I remember you from last year. You have a beard. And didn't I sit quietly in my room? There's no reason for him to do this to me. Excuse me, please, I can't seem to find my glasses . . ." Again her voice retreated from my ear, only this time not so far away that I could not hear her words melt into terse, hacking sobs.

"Please," I called into the mouthpiece, "Hello. Hello?"

"When you come here you won't see me." Her sobbing ceased abruptly and she was wheezing at me once again. "I will go up to my room. I do my music there. And I have my watercolors and my weaving. If he goes travelling, he should take me along. Are you downstairs? I could meet you at the door. Do you promise to speak to me first? I could tell you all you want to know."

"Perhaps you ought to tell me when your husband will be home."

"Never. Or a few minutes. He curses God. Who are you? Your voice is so faint. Are you downstairs?"

"I'm in my hotel. If you tell me when to call back — "

"Are you political? That's an important question. If you tell me that, I will tell you all. Of course, the Jews — "

" — "

"You don't know my husband very well, do you?"

"No, I don't."

"But you were here last year. We met downstairs. You had a beard. You were very young."

"Perhaps I ought to call back later. When your husband will be home."

"He doesn't live here anymore."

"He doesn't?"

"Are you downstairs or in your hotel?"

"I am in my hotel. Could you please — "

"Do you want to see my husband today?"

"Yes, I would, if that's — "

"He's dead."

"What? I'm sorry, I'm so sorry — "

"Are you religious?"

"I . . ."

"It doesn't matter. Please wait for me downstairs."

"I'm very sorry."

"Are you political? This has bearing on the question. When my husband comes home, he'll ask these questions. Please understand, I'm writing all of this down. Forty-five years is a long time to be someone's companion. Are you downstairs now? I thought I heard the door."

"I'm very sorry. I didn't know . . . " I was shaking with confusion. A moment before I had been hating this sad, crazy woman who stood between me and my goal. Suddenly everything had tilted, all had changed.

"Will you come and watch me pack his bags? I believe we know you from last year. Are you downstairs yet? I am in the room myself. Who are you? Can you help?"

Mustering my delicacy as well as my strength, I interrupted the rush of questions spouting from the telephone and asked one of my own.

"Is there someone else there I can speak to?"

"Oh, is that what you want after all? Explain to him about the years. Do you promise? If you do, I'll go to my room. I have music there, my weaving."

"I promise. Now please . . . "

"He just came back now. He went to the dry cleaners. I love you. Why do you ask me that? Here he comes. Years of weaving. Are you political? Do you have the right number? This is a Spanish-speaking household. Please report to the authorities — "

She stopped speaking and for a long suspended moment I could hear the sound of furniture scraping across a floor, the tinkle of shattering glass, and behind that the whir and whine of the city's eternal traffic jam both from the far side of the telephone line as well as from below my window.

"Who is this?"

A man's voice on the wire, the slightest touch of accent, like a daub of dark paint on a blank canvas, betraying his identity to me.

I hurried to explain myself and what I was after.

"How long has my wife been speaking with you?"

I fumbled for a reply.

"I apologize for her behavior. What is it that you want of me?"

I spoke as carefully as I could.

"I'm sorry. I don't give interviews anymore, Mister . . . " He mispronounced my name.

I spoke again, more slowly, trying not to plead.

"I am sorry."

"Your publisher — "

"He doesn't speak for me."

"Your letter — "

"My situation has changed."

"Your work — "

"My work speaks for itself."

"My project — "

"I'm very sorry. Please don't call here again."

Doves congregated on the rooftops, flapping their wings in protest against the metal-heavy air. From dozens of tubs and basins, boisterous water gushed, like sound through wires, setting the walls to trembling with its passage. Surprising me where I lay brooding in my solitude, the maid used her master key to enter my room. She apologized for intruding, bowing her head as she backed out the door. Later, the piercing shriek of rending steel, wailing sirens, voices shrilling in pain and dismay summoned as many of us as could hurry downstairs as witnesses to an accident other than our own.

Incidents of Travel
in the Yucatan

The small black mongrel sniffed about the crumbling, dusty stones, its paws clattering as it went.

"I can't imagine how it got up here."

"Some gringo, obviously."

"Why obviously?"

John Carter's girl leaned against the high pillar at the top of the pyramid called the House of the Dwarf, still recovering from the scare that had plucked at her on the climb. Although they had caught the first bus to the ruins and arrived to find no other tourists at the entrance to the site, she could have sworn she had heard a voice call to her in English while midway up the steep vertical steps, a voice that had distracted her from keeping her balance just long enough that she had nearly swung full around and pitched herself down the incline toward the rocks at the base. Carter had been no help. Blinking into the sun, he had not even noticed her distress. Regaining her precarious balance, she had rested on the step on which she had slipped, cursing the travel books he had given her for omitting any mention of the steepness of these ancient structures. What with loose stones, broken places, and the spots worn smooth by who knew how many thousands of previous climbers, there was danger here that she had not anticipated before she had reluctantly agreed to make the trek.

Carter patted the wayward dog. He had planned this trip both as a reward and a distraction for her, but ever since they had arrived it had seemed to her that he had made it a practice to climb faster, swim farther out, and always walk a few paces in advance of her — almost as if he were vacationing without her. On the far western border of the ruins, a weathered stone wall caught the early morning sun full on, its delicate filigree giving the appearance of a gigantic paper cutout planted by some enormous child among the flowering shrubs and runty trees. Here and there a moving figure at its base convinced her that they were not alone.

But the dog had already proved that. Perhaps it had been its master who had distracted her so dangerously with his call. It was nearing the end of the off-season, a good time to visit Yucatan. The last hurricane threat had faded and the great migration of North Americans from Houston and New Orleans had not yet begun. She winced at the thought that the dog had an American owner whom they would meet at some point along their climb atop the House of the Dwarf. Carter's guilt and embarrassment—or what she took to be those feelings—had made him suddenly ignorant of her own desires, but a wild man in the presence of other Americans. Whenever he saw a tourist on the street he would sneer and spit out derisive remarks in ungrammatical Spanish. In restaurants, he muttered about the ignorance of gringos who couldn't read the menus. This new boorishness went hand in hand with his changed attitude toward her. *He should be pampering me but instead he seems to want to ignore me.* He was a master at planning, she decided, but a failure at enjoying the execution of his plans.

The place of which I am now speaking was beyond all doubt once a large, populous, and highly civilized city, and the reader can nowhere find one word of it on any page of history. Who built it, why it was located on that spot away from water or any of those natural advantages which have determined the sites of cities whose histories are known, what led to its abandonment and destruction, no man can tell. The only name by which it is known is that of the hacienda on which it stands. In the oldest deed belonging to the Peon family, which goes back a hundred and forty years, the buildings are referred to in the boundaries of the estate as Las Casas de Piedra. This is the only ancient document or record in existence in which the place is mentioned at all, and there are no traditions except the wild superstitions of Indians in regard to particular buildings.

She ran her fingers along the rough, grainy surface of the stone against which she leaned and asked her question.

"What are you going to do about it, John?"

In the distance, unseen birds fluttered their wings and the noise echoed in the spaces between the antique buildings like the sound of peasant women shaking stiff, newly-washed sheets into the wind.

"I feel like a king or a wizard up here! This space, these buildings! Joan!"

He turned his broad back to her, peering out in the direction of the second large pyramid, a half-excavated structure that stood lower than the one which they had mounted only because of its location in a basin toward the southern end of the site. As he stretched his arms out in that direction, it seemed for a moment that he might attempt to leap out over the edge. Doves spurted up from the vegetation, as though startled by a stranger or a beast.

"Please answer my question! What are you going to do about the dog?"

Now he turned to face her, grinning broadly. He seemed to be pretending, arms still outstretched, that he belonged to some ancient Indian tableau, the giving of the law, the calling of the clans. His oval-framed, gold-rimmed eyeglasses and his finger-thick mustache that drooped at either end contradicted the message of his crudely-woven, rough cotton shirt and trousers. Gnarled, dusty toes poked out through his crude slippers made from the soles of outworn automobile tires. They might have belonged to any of the other passengers on the early morning bus that had carried them through the jungle. But his eyes glowed with the light of great cities in which he studied and worked.

Joan had been editing the moribund prose of a planner who believed that he was a writer. John had been working as a consultant in charge of a project that would regulate the flow of tourists in and out of the park system which the company was creating for a neighboring state. They had noticed each other in the office but not until her boss transferred her away from his speeches and into the parks project had they found the occasion to carefully look each other over.

"I'm a planner," he had introduced himself in the face of her somber but interested gaze, "and have I got a vision of a park."

The first object that arrests the eye on emerging from the forest is the building represented on the right-hand side of the engraving. Drawn off by mounds of ruins and piles of gigantic buildings, the eye returns and again fastens upon this lofty structure. It was the first building I entered. From its front doorway I counted sixteen elevations, with broken walls and mounds of stones, and vast, magnificent edifices, which at that distance seemed untouched by time and defying ruin. I stood in the doorway when the sun went down, throwing the buildings a prodigious breadth of shadow, darkening the terraces on which they stood, and presenting a scene strange enough for a work of enchantment.

The early part of her stay in the city had been marked by painful solitude. The frenzied childishness of the Macy's Thanksgiving Day Parade, with its bloated balloons depicting the familiar fantasies of her silly, lonely girlhood, had sustained her through her first such holiday away from her family. Depression set in before Christmas. Flying home had not helped her much. New Year's Eve in a hamlet on the outskirts of Evansville found her drunk, alone, at the site of her youth, talking to dolls. John Carter kept dolls, she discovered soon after her return to the city, brightly-painted ceramic figures dressed in garments of soft wool. They stood on the mantel of his working fireplace, souvenirs of trips to Greece — "to study the lintels of the Parthenon" — and the ruins of northern Mexico.

"I try to keep my commitments as spare as possible," he told her the night they went to bed. "I think that's why I like planning so much. It gives me pleasure to think that I can slim down the commitments of an entire populace. Fewer paces a day to broader horizons. Take a share of the future. Buy now, shop later. Got it?"

He raised a glass of smooth dry red wine, a variety she had never known existed while living among the bland diners of her home-town or the beer-glass smashers of the fraternities at State.

"Got it," she said, touching the bulging petal of her goblet to his.

We sat down on the very edge of the wall and strove in vain to penetrate the mystery by which we were surrounded. Who were the people that built this city? In the ruined cities of Egypt, even in the long-lost Petra, the stranger knows the story of the people whose vestiges he finds around him. America, say historians, was peopled by savages; but savages never reared these structures, savages never carved these stones.

He spoke only of the present, of the day's work, of the prospects for the evening's entertainment — which meant anything from a first-run film, to a vintage movie, a night in a jazz club on the fringe of Harlem, a photography exhibit at the headquarters of a large computer corporation. He spoke as an expert on many fields. She talked mostly about the past.

"I grew up in a small town and hated every minute of it. I felt like a changeling — "

"A what?"

At last, she discovered a subject, a fact about which he did not consider himself well-versed. She poured out her passions into a speech about changelings, their origins in myth, the implications of such for modern psychology, the nature of her own passionate attachment to the idea.

"Go on!" He punctuated her speech as though he were cheering a runner or a race horse.

"I was a stranger to my parents. I played by myself in my room, I read instead of embroidering and learning how to cook like the neighborhood girls. Of course I had my dolls, I started composing rhymes for them when I was six or seven, then stories. Want to hear one of the rhymes? 'Jack and Jill climbed down the hill/To fetch the pastor's daughter./Down down down, they went/Down down down!' Don't look so amazed! When you write something that silly, you remember it. 'Down down down.' I was really precocious. I hated school and I got my revenge by making the highest grades in the class and then refusing to acknowledge the honors. My parents scolded me. I learned how to fake a smile. I faked it until my cheeks ached. I smiled through years of feeling like a changeling. I smiled my way to the university, into a writing class, and smiled a recommendation from my instructor that I go east to the big city."

"You're not smiling now."

On the waterbed in the corner of his white-walled, Upper-East-Side apartment, she lay like a sacrifice to his feathered holiness, Heaven's Planner.

"That's because I'm feeling good."

"You frown when you're feeling good?"

"I stop my pretend smiling."

"You're a complicated lady, and I love you."

"What did you say?"

"I said, would you like to take a bike ride in the park?"

They rode on a ferry, they rode on a bus, they explored the city's subway line, they attended a poetry reading in a tropical-fish store, ate exotic food on the Lower East Side, and discovered that they both detested buttery French cooking. They discovered that they both enjoyed making love while Johnny Carson swatted at an imaginary golf ball with an imaginary club.

"Bizarre, eh?" he said. "Uh-oh, are you smiling?"

"I'm really smiling."

"How do I know the difference?"

"You'll have to trust me on this one, John."

He allowed her to play with his dolls.

These she used to strange advantage on nights when he would fall asleep over a mystery novel or fantasy adventure (his favorite kind of reading, she discovered, outside of planning journals), performing little playlets about an imaginary world she had called Lemuria after a lost continent in one of his books. On a piece of bond paper that glowed blankly under the dense beam of a Tensor lamp, she worked on a story about a war between two races of balloon creatures who lived on a continent invisible to all but a special variety of female child. Down down down, she chanted to herself as she raced to cover the paper with all of the drama that billowed suddenly in her mind.

There was an old woman who lived in a hut on the very spot now occupied by the structure on which this building is perched, and opposite the Casa del Gobernador *(which will be mentioned hereafter), who went mourning that she had no children. In her distress she one day took an egg, covered it with a cloth, and laid it away carefully in one corner of the hut. Every day she went to look at it, until one morning she found the egg hatched, and a* criatura, *or creature, or baby, born. The old woman was delighted; she called it her son, provided it with a nurse and took good care of it, so that in one year it walked and talked like a man, and then it stopped growing. The old woman was more delighted than ever, and said he would be a great king or lord.*

"If we can't find its owner, shouldn't we take it down?"

"Take it down?"

Carter smiled, but the space and light that surrounded them muffled the barking noise of his laugh.

"You mean you want *me* to carry the damned thing down those steps. With your vertigo, you wouldn't last a second."

One day she told him to go to the house of the Gobernador and challenge him to a trial of strength. The dwarf tried to beg off, but the old woman insisted, and he went. The guard admitted him, and he flung his challenge at the Gobernador. The latter smiled, and told him to lift a stone of three arrobas, or seventy-five pounds, at which the little fellow cried and returned to his mother, who sent him back to say that if the Gobernador lifted it first, he would afterward. The Gobernador lifted it, and the dwarf immediately did the same. The Gobernador then tried him with other feats of strength, and the dwarf regularly did whatever was done by the Gobernador.

Her vertigo! They had discovered it, while climbing the spiral metal steps within the hollow body of the Statue of Liberty, amid the cries and cheers and babbled comments of crowds of Puerto Ricans and other Spanish-speaking tourists, one of their Sunday excursions which had turned slightly grotesque. The feeling had hit her in the middle of the climb; he had been using that as a code for all of her hesitations ever since. Her vertigo! The last few months of work had been pure whirl, what with the rush to make revisions, the urgency of the delivery of the report. And then the event itself. Or the 'accident' as they had come to call it.

"Baby, I used to spill my food when I was younger, and bump into things a lot. I was black and blue most of my high school days. But once I got to college, I realized that I could cure myself of that nasty habit. I was trying to break myself into pieces. It's like most automobile crashes happen when somebody gets drunk and goes out for a spin."

She remembered his remarks all too clearly. She remembered the heat rushing to her face and the confusion when she realized that she had left claw marks from her fingernails where she had been holding onto the mantel above the fireplace.

"This was an accident. We used every bit of protection modern science has invented."

She stared into the face of one of the expressionless Greek dolls.

"Except abstinence, of course," she added, hurling herself back through years of time to those (now seemingly) splendid moments of isolation in her own place in her own room. Her hand reached instinctively for one of her dolls.

At length, indignant at being matched by a dwarf, the Gobernador told him that, unless he made a house in one night higher than any in the place, he would kill him. The poor dwarf again returned crying to his mother, who bade him not to be disheartened, and the next morning he awoke and found himself in this lofty building. The Gobernador, seeing it from the door of his palace, was astonished, and sent for the dwarf, and told him to collect two bundles of cocoyol, a wood of a very hard species, with one of which he, the Gobernador, would beat the dwarf over the head, and afterward the dwarf should beat him with the other. The dwarf again returned crying to his mother; but the latter told him not to be afraid, and put on the crown of his head a tortillita de trigo, a small thin cake of wheat flour.

"You're too smart and sexy to be a mother," he had said.

Something had turned and twisted inside her when he spoke, nothing that she had ever felt before until that moment of terrifying *absence* when it seemed to her that she had heard the call and nearly toppled backwards down the steep pyramid steps. She wept and wept, consulted a doctor, consulted friends, saw other doctors. This was the modern solution, everyone assured her. And yet she felt so antique and primitive in her sullen, swollen-faced response. Physically, her recovery was rapid. Her feelings toward Carter changed even as she healed. His boldness she began to hear as boisterousness. His impulsiveness she grew more and more to regard as bluster. As their work rushed toward a conclusion, prospects of changing her life tumbled through her head.

The trial was made in the presence of all the great men in the city. The Gobernador broke the whole of his bundle over the dwarf's head without hurting the little fellow in the least. He then tried to avoid the trial on his own head, but he had given his word in the presence of his officers and was obliged to submit. The second blow of the dwarf broke his skull in pieces, and all the spectators hailed the victor as their new Gobernador.

Joan's new dark mood had not gone unnoticed by him. On a day when she had left her office before him in order to do some research in a local university library, she returned home alone and found the apartment decorated with streamers and packed with friends. He had made chili for twelve to celebrate the conclusion of their project.

"Which means, friends," he said with beer glass raised on high, "that this little lady and I are going to be a-movin' on!"

"What's that, John?" she had asked, raising her head from her bowl of chili into which she had stared in order to keep her feelings to herself.

He reached under his place at the table and handed her a thick rectangular package. Their friends laughed and cheered.

"It's too early for Christmas," she said, digging in her heels against the festival mood as she carefully undid the bow around the package.

"It's not your birthday, is it?" asked one of their co-workers from the parks project.

She shook her head violently and applied a bit more strength to the wrapping.

"Wrong month!"

A cry went up from the guests as she discovered the smooth, glossy cover of the book.

Incidents of Travel in Central America, Chiapas & Yucatan, by John L. Stephens, Esquire.

"What's this for, John?"

"I thought you needed a vacation."

He beamed at her so aggressively that she nearly pitched the book at his face.

"So you got me a *book*?"

"Open it, baby!'

She obeyed his command.

"Oohh!"

She fingered the envelope before opening it, then slipped out the pair of airline tickets for all to see.

The old woman then died; but at the Indian village of Mani, seventeen leagues distant, there is a deep well, from which opens a cave that leads underground an immense distance to Merida. In this cave, on the bank of a stream, under the shade of a large tree, sits an old woman with a serpent by her side, who sells water in small quantities, not for money, but only for a criatura, or baby, to give the serpent to eat; and this old woman is the mother of the dwarf. Such is the fanciful legend connected with this edifice; but it hardly seemed more strange than the structure to which it referred.

The last few weeks in the city swirled about her as though she occupied the still center of a tropical storm. Finishing the project within the deadline pleased her. Nevertheless she hungered for important things left undone. One night, a few calendar marks away from their departure, she telephoned Evansville, something which she had only done before on birthdays anniversaries. The rapid clicks on the line as the phone call was connected distracted her for a moment from the tears that ran down her cheeks. As soon as her mother spoke, she realized that this was not the act she had to perform.

And how was John?

Fine, Mother. (John was her "fiancé" in their little family fiction, and their impending trip was "a shared vacation," as her mother had referred to it in a letter.)

Mom says you're studying up for your trip. Her father's voice yanked at something within her chest, as though he tugged on a rope attached to her lungs. Now that's the dandiest thing I ever heard.

Well, John gave me this fascinating book all about the ruins, Dad.

They had never met John but since he was a planner she had the feeling that they enjoyed his phantom presence. While her father talked a little about his own work (he was a highway engineer, and many a time they had crossed the Wabash by virtue of his technical expertise), she pictured the room where he stood, tiptoed down the hall past the bathroom and entered her bedroom. The dolls sat up in their usual places, the books showed their covers like hieroglyphics of her little-understood and long-departed infancy. Like an antique theater or a costume museum, the closet held clothing she had not worn in a dozen years. In the distance, down the carpeted hallway, she could hear her mother talking on the telephone.

The Casa del Gobernador stands with its front to the east. In the center and opposite the range of steps leading up to the terrace, are three principal doorways. The middle one is eight feet six inches wide and eight feet ten inches high; the others are of the same height, but two feet less in width. The center door opens into an apartment sixty feet long and twenty-seven feet deep, which is divided into two corridors by a wall three and a half feet thick, with a door of communication between of the same size with the door of the entrance. The floors are of smooth square stone, the walls of square blocks nicely laid and smoothly polished. The ceiling forms a triangular arch without the keystone . . . .

On takeoff, she had imagined them exploding, pieces of their lives tumbling down over the city. During the flight, she had lost herself in the Stephens, casting herself forward in time to such places as where she now stood. But nothing had prepared her for the vista of the ruins. Not even the vision of green islands flung across a turquoise sea, or the stone steps that led her eye from the coast down into the transparent waters of the Strait of Yucatan. She had felt flushed and excited ever since landing in Merida. If Carter hadn't suddenly lurched into his odd, new, aggressive mood, she would have had all of the necessary evidence for convincing herself that they had in fact done the right thing after all.

"Are you sure you can climb it, Joanie?"

"You're worried about my vertigo."

He looked about furtively, almost as if he were ashamed to be seen with her.

"I care about you, I worry about you."

"How sweet."

She had meant the words to come out light and gay. Irony instead weighed them down.

She had looked up then at the pyramid called the House of the Dwarf, and laughed bitterly. When she was a child she had shinnied up an apple tree, made a nest where two branches met, and then like a cat had sat until the rescue squad had arrived. She recalled her father's face when he had heard about it. A rope tugged at her lungs. The ground on which she stood seemed less firm than the steps which beckoned above her. There was a chain which guides had strung from top to bottom of the incline. Fearing immobility above all else, she reached out for it and pulled herself upward. How odd that an animal awaited her arrival!

The reader will be able to form some idea of the time, skill, and labor required for carving such a surface of stone, and the wealth, power, and cultivation of the people who could command such skill and labor for the mere decoration of their edifices. Probably all these ornaments have a symbolic meaning; each stone is part of an allegory or fable, hidden from us, inscrutable under the light of the feeble torch we may burn before it, but which, if ever revealed, will show that the history of the world yet remains to be written.

She slid around, her back to the open spaces between the ruined buildings, clutching at the creviced places in the outside wall of the little chamber.

Carter slid his arm around her waist, catching her before she could fall.

"Baby! Are you okay?"

She nodded, sniffing the acrid stone only inches from her nostrils.

"All of a sudden you just slumped over, like all the air went out of you."

"You're the one that's full of hot air!"

As though bursting paper bonds, she thrust her hands out to her sides and freed herself from his grip. Spinning about, she faced him squarely, wondering whether the blinking gaze he presented to her was the result of the sun—full and strong behind her in the east— or true surprise at her action. He reached for her again, but she slid away along the crumbling wall, as a lizard might or as a curtain might be drawn by a hidden hand.

"I want to go back to Merida now." She closed her eyes. Her heart fluttered like a bird poised for flight. Her bowels commenced to churn. This was not vertigo. This was something else and it burned her as it chilled.

"The dog," she added, fighting off the contractions.

"You don't let things drop, do you? All right, I'll take it down. Here, pooch, here boy, here perro! Perro, perro! And then can we at least take a look at the Governor's House?" He blinked the sun away again and disappeared behind the corner of the central chamber.

Joan followed him into the shade of the tower. Her stomach babbled just as it did for days following the operation. Sweat broke out on her forehead and she realized that she was squinting although the sun burned at her back. It was baking hot now outside the House of the Dwarf even in the shade, and she longed for nothing more than the shelter of their simple hotel room where two large ceiling fans whirled and whirled through the humid day and night and the cool tiled bathroom beckoned like a welcoming cave. She heard voices as she rounded the western corner of the chamber and at first she thought that he had at last found the owner of the beast. Then from below came a snort and a rumble, a tourist bus backfiring, a bitter shout, and the clop-clop-clop of figures in tire-soled sandals running at great speed, and she realized that they were still alone atop the pyramid.

I have now finished the exploration of the ruins. The reader is perhaps pleased that our labors were brought to an abrupt close but I assure him that I could have found it in my heart to be prolix beyond all bounds, and that in mercy I have been very brief; in fact, I have let slip the best chance that an author ever had to make his reader remember him. I will make no mention of other ruins of which we heard at more remote places. I have no doubt that a year may be passed with great interest in Yucatan. The field of American antiquities is barely opened; but for the present I have done.

She found him peering down the western slant where midway to the base the excavated steps turned smooth and silvery, like an ice slide on some wintry mountain in a state far to the north.

"Where is it, poor creature?" she asked.

The Quest for Ambrose Bierce

The bus rolled across the bridge to the south bank of the river and Alman breathed at last. He had imagined it to be a broader, swifter stream, but even so he felt newborn. Dark-faced boys in rags played among weeds and stubby cactus alongside the other shore. They didn't look up as he passed, but he waved anyway.

Oily fumes welled up inside the nearly-deserted bus as the vehicle slowed to a crawl and turned into a parking area at the rear of a group of low stone buildings. *Aduana.* Customs. *Immigracion.* Immigration. Alman flexed his college Spanish, a legacy that had finally convinced a doubting editor at *Ohio Magazine* to let him give this assignment a try. Inside one of the buildings a small dark man in an unpressed khaki uniform typed up his tourist card—"What for do you take in this machine?" he asked, pointing to the small portable typewriter Alman had bought at a Columbus discount store just before he departed. "You a journalist?" "To write letters home," Alman said with a straight face. The man nodded. "Not do it by hand?" He held up his hand, palm outward, as though showing Alman a secret sign. Alman shook his head. The man grinned and handed him his card. Alman had been warned about stating that he was entering the country in order to write an article. Nobody warned him about the smells, the noise, the sprightly music that rolled out of the loudspeakers in the small food stands on the edge of the parking lot.

"Señor?"

·The smiling, round-faced woman touched his arm just as he stepped into the next building for baggage inspection.

He backed away from her, but only far enough to get a good look at her breasts beneath her light synthetic sweater.

"Do you speak English?"

She smiled, as if approving his glance.

"I wan' hep. You give? I be you' mai'?"

"I don't need a maid."

She shook her head.

"Jes' for now, señor. For his 'spection."

"Oh?" Alman tried to figure out her plan. "You want to say you're my maid when you go through customs?"

"Si!" She showed him nearly every tooth in her mouth.

They were already walking slowly down the long corridor, their bags in their hands (and a sack slung over the chubby woman's shoulder as well). She didn't look like a drug smuggler or a prostitute. He nodded his agreement. The Mexican woman kept several paces behind him but he could feel her presence. He had a recollection of a news story about Mexican citizens bringing in appliances and new clothes from the U.S. and trying to avoid paying the duty. It was close to Christmas so he figured that this must be the case with the woman who wanted to pose as his maid.

A squat guard patted his typewriter, glanced inside his suitcase, listened to the woman's languid words about her service to this North American. Alman then found himself on the other side of the customs line.

"Gracias," she muttered as they returned to the bus. She placed her bulky sacks in the overhead rack alongside his typewriter and settled into the seat next to him.

He leaned away from her, giving her room to spread her billowy skirt. The woman—she told him her name was Marguerita Aceves after he introduced himself first—settled closer to him. Their thighs met, chaperoned by the folds of her skirt. The bus lurched forward through the desert twilight. Blue-black clouds hovered above distant mountains in the west. The last streaks of sunlight turned muddy beyond them. Joshua trees raised their stubby arms toward the darkening sky. Alman used unhappy memories of the past few lonely months as a sleeping pill. He dozed. Upon awakening, he found Marguerita Aceves' hand lying limply on his thigh. A minute passed in which he enjoyed the feel of her palm just above his kneecap. Then he edged toward the dark aisle. Moments later, her body sagged with the leftward movement of the bus, and her hand flopped back onto his leg, her head against his shoulder.

The bus roared like a dragon, approaching mountains on an endless incline of curves and more curves. It climbed and climbed into the high desert. Marguerita Aceves snored lightly in his ear. He imagined himself in bed with her, on top of her, married to her, raising her children. At least she smuggled for family and not just for herself. A faint tinge of heartburn swelled his breast at the thought of his own marriage in Columbus. But he didn't want to carry such excess baggage with him on this trip. And so he tried to imagine

Ambrose Bierce's bitter journey across the desert. And imagined leads for his article, his first but not, he hoped, his last.

Brap-ap-ap-ap-ap-ap! The bus expelled bad gas from its exhaust as it slowed down, steadying into a lower speed, then turning the curve that led westward. Alman must have dozed. Lights of a city flickered across his eyelids. Moments later the bus thumped along a roadway with special strips of concrete spaced out every few yards to slow them down. Alman shook off sleep and gazed at the lights of the bus terminal at the end of the long street.

"Permit me," said the awakening Marguerita, her voice fuzzy with sleep. He launched himself to his feet to allow her to pass down the aisle. As he watched her move lithely toward the door, he felt the heaviness in his bowels, thirst, heavy eyes. A few dark passengers from the rear brushed past him. Then he plunged after them into the aisle, into the terminal. In the brightly lighted but foul-smelling lavatory, he hurriedly unloaded his bladder and bowels, then bought a can of papaya juice and returned to the bus. Noxious engine fumes made it difficult for him to enjoy the sweet, thick juice of the tropical fruit.

Old passengers filed back into the vehicle, new ones arrived. A thin woman in black appeared at his side. He shook his head, telling her in signs that the seat was taken. Stoically, she passed on. Next a swarthy Indian peasant. More hand signals. The man protested. Alman sat up to full height. The man shuffled to the rear of the bus. Hurry now, he said to Marguerita Aceves in his mind. She ought to know better. These buses left on schedule. Broom — brooom ... The driver revved the engine.

He did not panic when the overweight man sat down. Sliding to the window, he searched the terminal yard for a glimpse of Marguerita. The bus bumped over the hump that slowed it down before the ticket window at the exit. Foreign chatter exploded around him, then subsided as the passengers settled down for the rest of the ride. No sight of her on the platform, he realized as he twisted around for one final look. He had not asked her her destination. He had not even known what contraband she had been smuggling. She had walked so lightly that it seemed that it must have been small cargo, perhaps even drugs or diamonds. The bus slowly rolled through the outskirts of the city, then plunged into the dark desert again at an ever increasing speed. Alman settled back, closed his eyes, rubbed his nose where the pain still tingled slightly, and tried to rehearse an outline for the article on Bierce. Not until he opened his eyes at the first touch of daybreak, as they slowed down once again amid vast tracts of grey and dun-brown dunes, did he discover that his type-writer was missing.

2

Armed with pen and notebook, Alman continued his search, a little bit wiser about his surroundings. His hotel room in Chihuahua was a perfect base — it was so dust-laden and depressing that he hated to return there. This encouraged him to spend hour after hour in the hall of records at the State capitol, and to take excursions into the countryside where lay the small villages frequented by the rebel soldiers of Villa during their campaign here in the north.

North? It was as far south as Alman had ever travelled, and the heat of noon on a winter's day convinced him that he didn't want to travel any further south, even in winter, if he could help it. But this was his story, and if it required that he follow tracks southward he would do so. Besides, he told himself, I might somehow meet up with that woman again and get my typewriter back. And he laughed at himself because he knew how naïve a thought that was.

Much to his own surprise, he accepted the rhythm of his new life in Chihuahua, a round of boring research, spicy meals, churning bowels, and lonely nights. Now and then he ate a new dish that pleased him — from time to time he heard himself making noises resembling laughter and others like cries of pain. No friends, no acquaintances cheered or annoyed him. He avoided calling Columbus although a few afternoons found him straying in the direction of the long-distance office. One morning an old man in the newspaper office showed him a yellowed sheet of newspaper with a story referring to the gringo journalist who was accompanying a villa-scouting expedition on an excursion to the coast. Alman was amused at how dislocated he felt when he left the city in the smelly, fuming third-class bus. He had been there only a week and a half but it had felt like home.

Pez de Espada. The name of his destination made him feel all the more uncertain. It was an ocean name — swordfish — and from his window he saw only desert, hour after hour nothing but flat sandy plain with a few distant mountains on the horizon. Only after dark did they begin to make their descent, and though he could not see much more than an occasional light in a peasant hut at the side of the thin highway, he felt the heat of the jungle rising up to meet him even as the bus spiralled its way downward toward the sea. By daybreak they rolled along a track under a canopy of palms and tall bushes, many of them heavy with red and yellow blossoms as large as his fists. The passengers who had boarded with him in Chihuahua trickled away stop by stop in tiny villages nestled along the downward-turning roadway. Few others boarded. By the middle of the night, Alman had the seat to himself. He had suffered, cramped up in the small space, but he had won some deserved sleep as well.

He awoke to discover the sea. The broad curve of the azure Pacific, sparkling in the morning light, punished him with its beauty. As the bus spiralled its way down through the welcoming jungle, he sweated beneath the same blanket that had kept out the chill during the night. Alman stripped it off. The bus rounded a turn in the jungle and a collection of palm-roofed hovels appeared down the road. Beyond them the sea burned with the fire of early morning sunlight. The bus driver spat out an oath.

The bus station was the only modern building in the village, a square stucco structure with posters plastered all over its outside walls and its waiting room laid with dirty tiles on which school children had painted a mural of butterfly-shaped fishing boats putting out to sea. From the ferocious glare of the sun, umbrellas, trees, stucco-roofed and -walled houses offered some surcease. But Alman had little time to worry about the heat.

An infant cried out. He glanced over his shoulder at a short, bulbous-nosed woman bundled up in a serape with an infant bulged against her chest. "Can you help me?"

Her voice was pure New York, so out of keeping with her appearance that Alman first looked around to see if someone else was speaking.

"Hello," he said, finally looking into her eyes. These were brown, as was the fringe of unkempt hair that hung down from beneath the hood formed by her serape. She had large cheeks, pocked and red, and her large nose was also cratered. Either her eyes were her only beautiful feature or they merely looked beautiful by comparison with her face.

"Can you help?"

"What's wrong?" Alman tried to catch a glimpse of the baby that the woman bundled so close to her body. Unlike the silent children he had seen on the streets of Chihuahua, this child made tiny mouse-like squeaks that penetrated the heavy cloth in which its mother had swaddled it.

"My name is Marsha." The woman blinked several times.

"Tommy Alman. Sounds like the nut."

"Tommy," she said, as though she had known him since grade school, "I need your help."

"What's wrong?" He swung his hand around and touched his wallet, an action that had become a habit since his encounter with Marguerita Aceves. Then he felt silly to imagine that he might be threatened by this dumpy American girl with her pathetic bundle of a baby.

"Help me get the bus to the border, I'm afraid to go by myself."

The woman trembled, and the cloth fell away from her head, revealing a tangled mess of dirty orange hair that was dark at the roots. She smiled feebly, yet invitingly, motioning toward the bundle of baby clothes heaped at her feet.

Alman paused a moment, as if thinking it over, but he was not truly thinking. In Columbus he had returned early from a trip to New York and had walked into his living room to find his wife in the arms of a stranger, and he walked out again, bumping his nose and shoulder against the door frame as he departed, returning to the office to demand an assignment and receiving the word about Bierce. Alman now picked up the bundle and headed to the ticket window.

3

He had made a number of stupid mistakes in his life, but they seemed nothing compared to the troubles of Marsha Meinrich, or Em, as she said her friends called her at college.

"I was an English major," she said, "but really I was into Latin-American stuff. Have you read —?" She named some authors whose names Alman didn't recognize. But then he had never read much; he had in fact never heard of Bierce until he had left the magazine office and stopped at a bookstore, found a couple of his books and then decided to take the bus south so that he had time to read them. He wanted to mention his assignment (or what had *been* his assignment, he had to admit to himself now that the bus took a curve that cut them off at last from the sight of the sea), but Marsha kept on chattering.

" — Teatro Boriqueño. Ever hear of that?"

"Sorry. What was that?"

"You weren't listening, Tommy. I said I met Enrique at the Teatro Boriqueño. The Puerto Rican Street Theater where I was an intern over the summer? He was one of the directors. He never went past eighth grade, but he read a lot of drama on his own and wrote some wild plays and also directed them. We were very simpatico, and I moved in with him on the Lower East Side. We had a really grungy place over on East 2nd Street, the part that looks like East Berlin but we loved each other and it didn't matter. Enrique was getting back to his roots, so I had to learn Spanish, which was really neat because even though I was away from him during the spring term, I felt close to him during the week because of my Spanish class, anyway it turned out I was pregnant and one of his things was his macho pride so that he didn't want me to get an abortion even though my parents were going crazy, and so I moved in with him at the end of the term. His family wanted us to get married, my family wanted an abortion, and I didn't know what I wanted except Enrique, so we got a little money together from friends and selling things and moved down here, not to Pez but to Oaxaca and then over here to Pez, the baby was born in Oaxaca and then Enrique decided he had to make some money and . . . "

They travelled for several hours while she put the story together for him, and he was as interested in the news about herself that she was giving him as in the terrain he had missed in the dark.

" — you know they bust you here for the smallest amount of anything, I mean, like aspirin without a prescription makes them look cross-eyed at you, it's a racket they use to shake down gringos, and I begged and begged him to stop carrying the stuff but he didn't listen and one day he was up in the city and bam, they picked him up and locked him in and except for a visit a couple of months ago, I haven't seen him . . . "

What an idiot that Enrique was! Alman wanted to tell her. But since it had taken her so long to get control of herself in order to tell him her story, he feared upsetting the balance she had regained. She had been through a lot of bad times and didn't need him to chip away at her feelings. If for no other reason than taking care of the baby, he didn't want her to become hysterical. Her plan was to cross back over into the States, call her parents, and then find a lawyer for Enrique. But what was his story? The bus rocked from side to side on the narrow highway through the jungle as he gave her an account of his own. Their hips bumped together and he told his tale in bits and pieces, wondering now and then about the lust he felt rising in his lap since she was such a striking picture of ugliness.

She wanted to stop in Chihuahua to buy some supplies for the baby.

"It's been weeks," she said, her voice returned to what was obviously its full strength, "since this little kitten has had clean diapers."

In the cool shade of the drug store, Alman volunteered to pay for the box of paper diapers.

"'Kleen-Bebe,'" she read from the label, "far out." Then she thrust the infant into his arms and announced that she was going shopping. "I'll meet you back at the bus station."

"What time?" he called after, the unfamiliar bundle squirming in his arms.

"When's the bus leave?" she asked over her shoulder.

He told her the time.

"I don't know anything about what to do with this!"

"It's good practice!"

She waddled off along the sun-bleached avenue, leaving him the object of curiosity of a number of admiring pedestrians. The infant had calmed down, but now he realized that it was giving off a sweetish but repugnant odor. Wandering back toward the bus station, he spied a small park and lay the baby down on the grass, letting it kick and make fists at the trees. He undid its filthy wrapping, marvelling that a few thin streaks of excrement could emit such a foul smell. He daubed carefully at the boy's genitals with his handkerchief — which he then rolled up into a ball and left lying at the base of a tree — and after ruining the tapes on only two diapers, successfully negotiated the change.

Vendors approached them, asking him to buy slices of fruit or vegetables, roasted seeds and nuts. He didn't feel hungry although he hadn't eaten in half a day. When the infant stopped its silent calisthenics and slept, he dozed off only to be awakened by a pinch on his neck and another on his cheek. A scouting party of red ants had attacked him, and as he brushed them aside, he remembered the baby. But the thing slept peacefully, apparently invulnerable to the marauding insects.

"Hey!"

Alman looked up to see Marsha kicking the grass in front of him with the toe of a cowboy boot. She wore a western shirt, faded jeans, and her hair was pulled back to show off all the more starkly the jutting ugliness of her nose and the craters of cheeks. But now that she had shed her serape, he could see a nicely-shaped body that distracted him from the unpleasantness of her face.

"Where'd you change?" Alman asked, sitting up and then scooping up the baby in his arms.

Marsha smiled. "You look good with the kid, man. I met a friend of Enrique's. He let me clean up in his place."

"You should have taken the baby with you," Alman said. "It smells."

Marsha relieved him of the child.

"Can't face up to the essential odor of the human race, can you, man? I thought we were supposed to meet in the bus station. I was looking all over for you."

"You didn't think I'd run off with him, did you?"

He stood up and they started walking toward the station, Alman slinging her bags over his shoulders, Marsha with the baby in her arms.

"Actually I think you'd be very good with it." She smiled slyly.

Alman thought she was taunting him and ignored her look. They had missed one bus to the border and now had an hour to wait for another. While Marsha sat on a bench with her blouse open and nursed the baby, he went out to buy them some food for the trip.

Darkness settled over the desert by the time they rolled north out of the flat dry city. El Paso, their destination, lay hours away across the dunes. Marsha, in the window seat, asked him to hold the baby while she ate, and then did the same for him. The food was peppery, but the milk nicely cooled his burning tongue.

"He'll sleep all the way," Marsha said, "and I'll change him just before we cross the border so that he doesn't make a mess while we're in customs. Like I once got stuck there for hours one time with Enrique, man, and the baby nearly went berserk."

"Is that where he got caught?"

"Huh? Oh, yeah, but not at the border. He was driving along in Sinaloa and ran into a roadblock. What a bad break, man. They wanted to crucify him and now he's rusting away in prison." There was something in her voice that disturbed him.

"I hope you're going to try and do something for him once you get home."

Marsha had been bumping shoulders with him as they rode. Now she pulled herself toward the window.

"What kind of a chick do you think I am?"

Alman retreated as far as he could toward the aisle.

"I don't know, Marsha, it just sounded like . . . "

"Let me tell you, everything isn't always the way it sounds. And that's not something they teach you real well in college. Tommy

Nut, you think it's time to get aggressive with me? Now I know exactly why your wife left you."

The remark hit Alman in the chest like a fist.

"Why was that?"

"Because you pretend you're macho when you're really just a pushover."

Marsha burped loudly, adjusted the sleeping baby in the crook of her arm as though the infant were a limp-limbed rag doll, closed her eyes, and went to sleep.

A large bright moon dominated the desert highway. Alman would have liked to have blamed its piercing light for his own inability to sleep, but he knew that what kept him awake were the facts of his life rolling about in his brain like loose luggage on the upper rack of the bus. Without even feeling very sorry for himself, he understood that up until now his days had simply caved in on him, like sand in a pit in the desert through which the bus now carried him. He had no momentum of his own—having staggered out of his family home and college days he finally had slowed down and fallen over. His marriage, or the end of it, marked the place where he tipped over and stopped running. Though he was rolling north toward the border of his country and knew absolutely nothing about what he would do once he got there, he prayed that he would find something. Something. Something. To the tune of his seatmate's stertorous breathing, finally he dozed.

More than a moment but less than an hour had gone by when he opened his eyes. The moon had slipped down behind them, and the bus roared forward toward Texas and darkness. Either the baby or the woman had stirred, rousing him from his slumber. When he moved slightly in the seat, he felt the heel of a hand resting on his upper thigh while the fingers worked open the zipper of his corduroy trousers.

He glanced over at Marsha, but she lay back, eyes closed, the baby still asleep on her arm, as though she knew nothing about the stealthy steady progress of her own hand. Suddenly she had the zipper unlatched, and spread open the metal teeth. Like a ferret after a rabbit, her hand swiftly entered the slit in the front of his undershorts and grasped his flaccid penis.

The shock pressed him back against the seat, and he rolled his eyes about, fearing that some full-bladdered passenger might this very moment stumble down the aisle toward the bathroom in the rear of the bus. But no one stirred; only the fuss and roar of the engine, and the thumpedty-thud of the tires on the bumpy desert highway, broke the silence that encircled him like her fingers tightening around his organ. It was a dream, it was a fantasy out of the pages of a magazine, it was a dilemma, it was a pleasure, it was a tricky quickening sense of the improbable taking place right there in his own lap, a daydream at night, a surging, mounting, thickening, a blurring of sight and urging of feeling, a bucking of his hips; he spurted into her hand.

No less quickly than she had found him, she pulled away, sliding her slick fingers across his thighs. She wiped them on the baby's blanket, and withdrew back into the sleep that she had surprised him from, like a sea animal retiring into its shell. Alman, lulled into a stupor, closed his eyes, listened to the bus, remembering only when he noticed the shape of another passenger against the darkness of the aisle that he had to adjust his trousers.

He must have slept because a faint touch of light dappled the horizon just beyond the supine girl's shoulder. He was glad that she hadn't awakened because it gave him a minute to decide how to treat the whole thing when she opened her eyes. As it turned out, he needed no strategy. When in the next few moments the bus swerved to avoid a cow grazing at the roadside, Marsha sat up, bright-eyed, and inquired after the time. When he told her, she beamed.

"We're almost to the border," she said. "Don't you need to take a piss or something? I want to stretch out and change the baby."

He nodded, pleased that nothing of their encounter in the darkness showed in her eyes. He got up, and she immediately set down the sleeping infant on his seat, reaching into her knapsack for a fresh diaper. The stench inside the tiny bathroom nearly made him gag. But he took advantage of the small sink with the pump faucet to wash himself. When he returned to the middle of the bus, Marsha was nursing the baby whose tiny birdlike noises spoke of hunger unlike any he had known in a long while.

The moon had departed, the sun lolled up over the dunes. Within minutes he could make out the towers and rooftops of Juarez with El Paso on the northern bank of the winking river. In a few more minutes, they were rolling past shacks made of corrugated tin, and then small brick houses with dry front yards full of cactus trees and bluebonnets. They had to switch buses at the Juarez station for their trip across the border. With its odor of insecticide, whiskey, cigarettes, and body odor, the ancient vehicle that carried them onto the bridge might have been the same one that had transported him southward only a few weeks ago. Except that this time no dumpy Mexican women looked nervously about as they approached the customs checkpoint. Only a few laborers who had boarded in Juarez accompanied him and Marsha into the U.S. customs building at the side of the broad cement bridgeway.

A dour Mexican official collected their tourist cards — and then motioned for them to move on to American territory. There a uniformed Texan, narrow as a reed, looked him in the eye, asking if they had anything to declare.

"No, sir," Alman said.

"Open these, please," the official said stiffly, rummaging through Alman's small suitcase and Marsha's knapsack.

"How old's the baby?" he asked.

Alman said, "Uh..."

"New fathers!" Marsha broke in with a snort, telling the man the infant's age in months.

The man kept on feeling about in the knapsack, but his voice took on a more gentle quality than the movement of his hand suggested.

"That all you have with you, son?"

Alman nodded.

"I had a typewriter but it was stolen."

"That's the way it is down there," the official said, as though he were talking about a pit or the ocean bottom. "Okay, you can get back on the bus now."

"Thank you, sir," Alman said. Marsha remained silent as they left the customs booth and reboarded the reeking bus. When they were turning down a short street that led to the El Paso Greyhound Station, she said, quietly, "You're terrific."

Alman had no idea what she meant, and was still too embarrassed about the incident in the night to ask about it. At least one thing had become clear: he wasn't going to go back to work for the magazine, and that was fine with him.

"Baby needs a change," Marsha declared when the bus came to a stop.

"I'll do it," Alman volunteered, pulling their luggage down from the rack and following her out of the bus and into the depot. They had a number of benches to choose among in the nearly deserted station. Marsha selected one in the corner by the baggage room which at this hour had not yet opened. She spread a blanket on the bench and gently lay the infant of top of it.

"Listen, you check the time of the New York bus, okay, honey? I'll change the baby."

"Honey?" Alman saw that she was about to pull open the child's diaper. "Okay." He ambled over toward the ticket counter where the schedule was mounted on a board in white plastic letters and numbers. New York? Why New York? Her husband was in jail in Mexico. Why did she want to go all the way up to New York? Maybe he could convince her to go somewhere else. She seemed quite footloose for all of the needs of the baby. He checked the time of the next bus to New York but also of the next one to Los Angeles. He'd only been there a few times selling space, but it was a new town and maybe a better town for him, or them, than New York.

"I'm just going to get rid of this poo-poo," Marsha said when he returned to the bench. She held up at arm's length a neatly-folded diaper.

Alman nodded, sitting down alongside the infant who seemed to be asleep again and watching Marsha walk slowly off in search of a place to dispose of the loaded diaper.

She folds a diaper nice, he thought, you'd think even the kid's shit was precious. He decided that he would try to talk her out of going to New York and into trying another town, maybe L.A. or Houston, he had sold space in Houston, too, and it was a growing town. You don't want to go all that far away from your husband, do you? he'd say. Think of the baby, he'll want to see the baby. I'll convince her. She probably only wants to go to see her own family a while and then come back down. He remembered what she did for him in the dark of the bus. We'll stop, we'll take a hotel room. He pictured all kinds of pleasure for them in the dark room. When you came right down to it, her face wasn't all that bad, and besides she was a good mother. Honey, she had called him. Tommy the Nut. He listened to her voice in his mind.

A bus full of workers from the other side of the river unloaded noisily, filling the depot with Spanish and cigarette smoke. Alman stood up and looked around. She's in the ladies, he decided. He sat down.

A second bus load of workers arrived. The ticket seller opened the booth, illuminating his sign with a flick of a switch. Alman poked around in the knapsack, found that it was full of paper diapers and small bottles, cans of powdered milk, clothing. A policeman appeared in the center of the depot, and when he strolled near the bench, Alman, for some reason he could not explain, turned to look after the baby.

The ticket seller called out the times of departing buses. When Alman heard the New York bus announced he picked up the sleeping infant, amazed as before at its near weightlessness, and hurried outside into the light of full dawn. She wasn't anywhere in sight. He rushed back to check the gate where a small group of dark-skinned travellers shuffled in toward the bus.

"New York?" asked the driver at the gate.

Alman shook his head, retreating to the bench.

"Jesus," he muttered. He waited on the bench a while longer, then scooped up child, knapsack, and his own suitcase, and walked to the ticket counter. "Did you see?" The baby stirred, and he rocked it gently in his arms, hoping that it would remain asleep.

"Is a boy?" The brown-skinned ticket seller looked at him blankly.

Alman nodded.

"What's it call?"

Alman shook his head.

Later, as they departed for Las Cruces, with the morning sun behind them, Alman, hands trembling, heart beating wildly despite the calm and certitude of the humming American bus, patted the wailing infant on its bottom until its noisy fears subsided.

In Tucson, amidst the ammoniac fumes of the men's room, he changed the infant yet one more time. In Phoenix, after picking a cigarette butt from the drain, he sat the naked creature in the sink, bathed it with a paper towel and rubbed it with ointment he found in the knapsack. Dabbing water on its brow, he took a deep breath and gave the child an old-fashioned masculine name.

Fishing for Coyotes

In an East Texas bus station on Christmas Eve day a delicate-appearing young woman with a ruddy face and sandy hair, an infant in her arms, steps down from a dust-streaked Greyhound. Next out of the bus is her husband, a tall man slightly older in appearance, with a shock of thick black hair. He carries a suitcase and wears several shoulder bags bulging with clothing.

"You know you can do your sketch when we get to their house," the woman says. "Uncle Ben is probably waiting for us." She leads the man into the waiting room, looks around, and heads out through the street door, hugging the baby close to her chest even though Corpus Christi feels only a few degrees colder than the town to the south where they boarded the bus the night before. Having spent her childhood here, she knows that at Christmas a storm can blow up out of nowhere, and so she has come prepared.

"If it's O.K. with you, I think I'll sit down and try to start it until he gets here," her husband says.

The woman—her name is April—searches the roadway that runs along the beach, leading down to the bay.

"I see him!" she says, the relief showing in her voice. "It *is* him. Uncle Ben! Hi! We're here!" she calls out, although there is no chance that the man behind the wheel of the large blue car can hear her. But he sees her, and waves back. She glances at her husband and down at the sleeping child. She doesn't want two infants on her hands—not with all of their luggage and a Christmas holiday with her mother to deal with. When her uncle, a huge man who has to work himself slowly out from behind the wheel of the car, waddles up to them, she rushes forward with the baby and throws herself into his arms.

"Your mama's going to do a cartwheel when she sees this little thing, honey," Ben says, and his voice booms in the parking lot. "We all been looking forward to meeting you, William." He thrusts a beefy hand past April's shoulder and shakes her husband's fist. "Hear you're a artist."

"That's right," William says, "but you can't tell too easily, because I shaved my beard."

April steps back from the two men, enjoying the presence of this uncle who is a bloated version of the father she remembers, a newspaperman who wrote for the East Texas daily where Ben still runs the pressroom.

William narrates the saga of his Mexican haircut and shave while they load their belongings into the trunk of Ben's car. A few spins of the wheel and they are rolling along past the harbor, where a row of new motels mars April's vision of the beach of her childhood. Small fast-moving clouds with bright fringes and dark undersides mark the horizon where the bay meets the Gulf. The weather is just as she remembers it—a mixture of promise and menace.

By the time they arrive at the small brick ranch-style house on the outskirts of town, William seems to have forgotten that he was angry that she wouldn't let him sit down right away and sketch the sunrise he had seen from the bus as they crossed the border into Texas. He assists April with the baby while Ben attacks the luggage. But no one can help April with the fear that arises when she enters the house.

In the narrow foyer, she catches the scent of her mother's whiskey breath and chokes at the smell. But when her mother appears in front of her, suddenly old, her hair gone all silver, the choking becomes a sob. April opens her arms to her mother and clasps her around the shoulders the way she has seen prize fighters do on television. The women weep in each other's arms.

Ben ambles up alongside of them holding the baby. "Where do I put this package, lady?"

April's mother frees herself from her daughter and snatches up the child as though saving it from a fire. "I d-don't even remember her name!" she says with a wail.

"Marina, Mama. It's from Shakespeare. Don't scare her now with your crying."

Aunt Sal, Ben's wife, dark-complected, her hair heaped up on her head like a pile of leaves, comes over to greet April with a whiskey kiss.

"And here's the man responsible," Ben says, nudging William toward Sal.

Husband and aunt shake hands, unable to find much to say to each other. They glance at the child, who is now alert, dribbling sounds down her chin.

"You must be real tired from sitting up all night on the bus," says Sal, who has been April's mother's landlady ever since she sold her small rancher and moved to town.

"I hope we're not going to be too much trouble," April says.

"No trouble at all," says Sal, taking her first full look at William, who is interpreting for April's mother the sounds coming from Marina. "Just you and your mama keep out of each other's hair and we'll have us a big old Christmas."

"You're getting along O.K.?" April asks, her voice a whisper.

"I enjoy keeping your mama, and she enjoys being kept."

And it is true that in the next hours there seems to be little friction between the women.

"It's only between me and Mother that the sparks fly," April says to William later, in the afternoon, when they have been relieved of baby duty and installed, for a "nappie," as Sal calls it, in a bedroom far to the rear of the house.

"How about some friction between us?" William says in the tone he must have used on all of the women he brought up to the loft before their marriage, a tone she once found irresistible.

"This won't help at all," April says, batting aside his groping hands. But they lie beneath the covers, and only faint sounds of laughter reach them through the thick, locked door. What happens next seems to her as inevitable as the romance that followed their meeting on a Seventh Avenue downtown local, and the marriage that followed the romance, and the baby that followed before the year was out.

They awake into Christmas Eve. Ben has invited April to come outside while he lights the luminarias — stubby white candles stuck into sand at the bottom of paper sacks. It is a custom that she had forgotten. But, standing at her uncle's side, she recalls how when she was a child she enjoyed this little ceremony, and how later, just after she entered high school, when her father was already ill and her mother drinking steadily, she and some friends walked past house after house kicking over the neat rows of glowing orange sacks.

"Tell me about that newspaper job," Ben says, tamping down the sand in those sacks unprotected from the breeze by the hedge or the line of shrubs.

"How did you hear about that?"

"You listed me as a reference. They called me."

April frowns, still a little surprised that a newspaper would care that much about her application. At college in the North, she had never paid much attention to the campus paper, let alone written for it. But after graduation, when she realized that she was either going to have to find work or return home, it occurred to her that she ought to apply for a newspaper job in New York City. At the time, what had drawn her to her father's profession was its loose hours and the prospect of seeing her name in print. Now she remembered a saying of his, one that she had repeated to herself over and over again during the subway ride up to the office of the *Times* on that lonely first day in New York—"Every story worth its bacon opens with a hook." Making it seem as if that was all there was to it.

The wind shifts and April kneels, using her body to shelter a sack as she lights the candle inside it. "They eventually offered me a job as a copygirl, Uncle Ben, but I had to turn it down. I was pretty far along with Marina by then. Anyway, we had already found out about the school in Mexico where I'm teaching. We decided it would be the best thing for both of us if I do this kind of work for now—while William paints. *The New York Times* just called me too late, I guess."

Uncle Ben cups his meaty fist around a cigarette and lights it with the same ease with which he ignites the candles in the sacks. He puffs on the cigarette and the wind scatters sparks across the lawn. "You like teaching those diplomatic brats?"

"Nothing I want to do for the rest of my life. But for now it's O.K., Uncle Ben."

"Have time to enjoy your baby down there?"

"We have a sort of maid-babysitter. She comes in while I go to school." Anticipating his next question, she adds, "William works in his studio at home."

"He sell things?"

"He's just getting started, Uncle Ben. He's got a little money that comes in from an aunt who died last year."

"Nice going. When your Aunt Sal passes, she'll leave you the recipe for her barbecue sauce."

"He's not rich at all," she assures him.

"No," Ben says, "not if you come on the bus. Was it a good ride? I ain't been down that way for years."

April thinks back to the dark desert road, the baby and William asleep while she stared out into the blackness in fear of her meeting with her mother. "It was O.K."

"But nothing you want to do for the rest of your life."

They laugh, then move along to light the remaining candles. When they are finished, Ben hugs April and she feels his barrel chest against her, big as the whole state of Texas.

Inside the house, the drinking has already begun.

"What a nice young man this is!" Aunt Sal declares. "I'm so sorry he shaved his beard! I wanted to see how a real artist looks!"

"I told Sal we didn't want to have any hassles at the border," William says.

April catches a glimpse of her mother pouring herself another Scotch. Then, before she knows it, she has had three to drink herself, and she stops thinking about anything except sweet little Marina, who sleeps peacefully in the rented crib in a room down the hall from their own. William, under the direction of Sal, now gathers together the pails he and Ben will need when they drive over to the Mexican side of town to pick up the tamales for the Christmas Eve supper. She is pleased that William is having such a good time — she knows he must be, since he's made no further mention of his sunrise sketch.

She doesn't feel abandoned, the way she often does when William leaves her with the baby. Her mother and aunt appear much more benign than she remembers. If Marina wakes up, they will help her, she feels sure. It's a miracle that the baby doesn't wake, their voices ring so sharply through the room. They're talking about old times — many buckets of tamales ago, as Aunt Sal puts it. April's mother doesn't protest. She takes a sip of her Scotch and sags forward, as though someone had let the air out of her, head on chest. In a moment, she is snoring.

"She just loves being a grandmother so much, " Sal says. "She made a promise to herself — no more quarreling with you."

"She'll just pass out, instead."

Sal purses her lips and touches them to the rim of her glass. "I guess nothing much happened to you up north except you got yourself a husband and a baby."

April stares at her aunt until the woman finally lowers her eyes and sips her drink. "How's Arvin? Still selling Coke?"

"Your cousin is doing just fine. He opened one of those drive-in food restaurants up in Lubbock, and he's making himself a nice living. He's working tomorrow — only place in town open on Christmas. Figure he'll make a week's money in one day."

"That's nice," April says, trying to keep scorn for her big-eared first cousin from showing in her voice.

After a long silence, her aunt asks, "How come you turned down that good job?"

April sits up nervously, glancing over at her slumbering mother. "Did she ask you to find out for her after she passed out?"

"Aw, honey, I was just wondering. They called your Uncle Ben, you know."

"He told me," April says.

She excuses herself and attempts to walk a straight line for the bathroom down the hall, but bounces off one wall and then the other. "Like mother like daughter," she tells herself with the same scorn that crept into the question about her cousin. Before she knows it, she has turned on the bathroom faucet. She undoes her slacks. She could be five years old again. But when she is ready to return to her aunt, a look in the mirror on the medicine chest reassures her that she's herself, a ruddy-cheeked, sandy-haired, green-eyed twenty-three. She flicks her tongue across her lips as though she were about to step into a room full of New York partygoers where she might meet the man of her life. Then, as she joins Sal in the living room, she hears her father laugh.

It is Ben laughing. He and William have returned with the tamales.

The rest of the evening slurs by. With her knees pressed against the edge of a plastic TV tray, April takes her first bite of the traditional midnight supper and tells William that she feels like Proust's Marcel.

"Who?" he asks drunkenly. Then he says, "Oh, yeah."

Outside the window, paper sacks go up in flames as the wind shifts off the bay. April's mother sits up long enough to bid everyone Merry Christmas and to all a good night. Ben and Sal soon excuse themselves, leaving April with a William suddenly morose.

"The sketch," she says.

"You can read my mind."

Then he slinks off to bed and she's listening to the house quiet down. Suddenly she leaps to her feet and rushes down the hall. Sure enough, Marina has awakened. April changes her in the crib, picks her up, and, pacing the room, rocks her back to sleep. She attempts to exhale her whiskey breath away from the baby's face, but it is hopeless. How many nights did her own mother spray her with the sweet metallic whiskey droplets of her breath? She paces and rocks and she knows how difficult it was for her mother to do anything else.

"Merry Christmas!" April's mother, baby in arms, surprises them in bed. Shaking off sleep, April peers through blurred eyes at her mother's bright face.

"What time is it?" Her voice sounds crackly and parched, the way her mother's voice ought to sound but doesn't.

"Later than you think! Arvin called early, woke everybody up. I've been to church already."

"Jesus!" William says from beneath the covers.

"Blasphemer!" April's mother calls to him, half serious.

"Who took care of Marina while you . . . ?"

"Ben and Sal. Come on up, you-all. We're heading out for the picnic."

April collects herself. Her mother has made such a remarkable recovery she thinks there might be hope for her. She nudges William, who reeks of last night's fiesta. He burrows deeper into the covers. In the shower, she raises her arms as if surrendering to a lawman and lets hot water pound away at her back.

"Where's this picnic again?" William asks as they trundle out to the car—the two of them, April's mother with baby in arms, Ben and Sal carrying baskets of food.

"On Padre Island," April replies, trying to make sense of the feeling of great warmth that overwhelms her at the sight of her mother holding little Marina. Her mother hasn't had a drink yet and it's two hours since breakfast. Sal bumps hips with April when William holds open the rear door of the car, and motions for April to slide onto the seat.

"I'm sitting next to this gal," she says, "'cause I still got some unanswered questions."

April sits behind Ben, who drives the large Buick as though it were a motorboat, swaying from one side of the road to the other, following mysterious patterns of waves on the highway leading south. William looks through the window at the flat land stretching out in all directions. In the front passenger seat grandmother and baby make noises at one another.

Sal asks April how she and William met.

"On the Seventh Avenue downtown local just after I'd come back from applying for that job at the *New York Times*," April says.

Sal asks her about their wedding: a ceremony they wrote themselves in William's downtown loft. "Everything's downtown in New York City. At least, that's how it seems to me," Sal says. "You know how unhappy we all were that we couldn't come up for it, but Ben had to work and your mama, she just wasn't feeling well at the time. And then along came that beautiful little critter, that Marina! We sure wished we were up there to see when she arrived!"

"Maybe we can all stay in better touch from now on," April says. "Life up North gets kind of . . . disconnected from family things . . ."

"Hey!" says Ben from behind the wheel. "How come you let them Yankees beat your accent out of you!"

"I like her accent," William says, his first words of the entire ride. "I want her to keep it."

"He shinks it's cute," Aunt Sal says, slurring her words as though she'd had a few drinks. But April can smell her breath—it's pure coffee and cigarettes and eggs and bacon.

"This is cute," says April's mother from the front seat, holding aloft a smiling Marina.

Padre Island 3. April shivers at the sign. She begins to explain the family tradition to William, but Sal takes over and it's just the way it was when April was a little girl, "Buster—that's Ben's brother, April's daddy—they used to come out here every Christmas morning with their daddy; he came all the way from Tennessee when he was a boy; now, he was a newspaperman himself...."

The car swings into a left turn onto the causeway connecting mainland to island, and they sway from side to side like passengers on the deck of one of the small steamers April can see on the horizon of the looming slate-grey gulf. She thinks of the poor sailors, of how they must feel to be on the sea instead of in port at a time like this, when any port would pass for home. The thin strip of sand dunes stretches out before them north and south—like the bent bow of a giant Indian hunter up to his waist in the middle of the gulf aiming a huge arrow at El Paso, far to the west, she once wrote in a school essay, a piece of writing her father found so pleasing that he quoted from it in his column.

"There'll be some nice places where you can sketch," she says over Aunt Sal's lap to William.

"Um," he replies, lost apparently in the vista of low dark-bottomed clouds that lead the way, like stepping stones across a creek, toward the Mexican border.

There's a sudden shift in the car's swaying motion, and the wheels whir in the sand. As Ben turns right and rolls them a short distance down the beach, April wonders idly what it would be like to head directly into the knee-high breakers so that the car was stuck in the sand while the tide rolled in. Marina's cry yanks her from this vision.

"Please cover her head, Mama," she says as they prepare to disembark.

"I think I remember how to take care of a little one on this beach," her mother replies, an edge to her voice which April hasn't heard for years.

"Please," April says, concerned when she opens the door and feels the full blast of the sea wind on her face.

"Come help us," Sal breaks in, alert to the danger of a quarrel. "We got to set this up real quick and get a fire started. William?"

"He wants to do some sketching," April says. "Anyway, I'll do his share over here. You go on, Will."

She sees how her husband admires the sea birds hanging motionless above the breakers. The cries of the gulls blow in with the stiff breeze that keeps them suspended, their beaks pointed toward the turquoise sky to the east, a thin strip of light where the cloud cover falls short of the horizon.

"Sunny in Florida," Ben says, unloading chairs and kettles and bottles and boxes from the trunk of the car as though rescuing heirlooms from a fire. April, unfolding beach chairs, figures that she might as well be niece to a marlin as to this huge man. His life, his motives remain a mystery to her. She can tell by his grin that he's drunk already. What if he didn't bear any resemblance at all to her father, she thinks—would she love him as much then? She brushes her hair out of her eyes, turns to see how William is doing. He has wandered off southward along the dunes.

"Sunny in Mexico, too," she says.

Her uncle looks up from pulling out the last box from the trunk and motions for Sal, who has been waiting at the open rear door of the car.

He is ready for her to do her part.

"How's it living down there with the Messkins?" he asks April.

"Just like living up North with the snow diggers. I try to be myself and get along with everybody. It's a nice life for the baby so long as we can keep her healthy."

Sal brushes past April and joins Ben over the small platform he has erected in the sand. A yellow-tipped flame leaps unexpectedly above the rim.

"Magic," says April.

"Sterno," says Ben. "Don't you remember?"

"Sure do," April says, and she glances toward the front of the car, where she thinks she hears the baby. But it is a gull shrieking into the wind out where the breakers begin.

"Don't look now, honey," Sal says, touching her arm. "Your Southern's coming back. Hey, where's that artist husband of yours? Isn't he going to want some steak?"

"May be against his religion," Ben says. "I hear tell artists are supposed to starve." He slaps himself on his imposing stomach. "Guess I'll just be a laborer in this life. Your daddy, now, there was an artist who could be a laboring man at the same time."

April peers up into the wind, as hungry for news about her father as she is for the steak now sizzling on the makeshift grill.

"Was he, Uncle Ben?" She hears it in her voice, and she is sure Ben hears it, too—the pleading near whine of a young girl wanting a story before bedtime.

"Come round these parts more often and I'll tell you plenty, April."

April smiles politely. There's a feeling she has, a question she wants to ask, but something catches her eye down the beach, a dark flicker above the water too low to be a leaping fish, too high to be a skimming bird hunting for its holiday brunch. Whatever it is, it's gone.

Ben is speaking, but his words whip away like ashes from the tip of his smoldering cigarette.

Abruptly, April turns to look behind her. Nothing there but the gulf. She's trembling now. It doesn't please her to be back on this beach — lured by William into marriage, lured down to Mexico to take a job she didn't like, tempted back across the border by the need to feel like family. Marina is the only real choice in her adult life that she can call her own. And Marina was an accident.

Ben has stopped talking. Excusing herself, April walks over to the car. There, in the front seat, she spies grandmother and granddaughter sleeping. Satisfied with the sight, she walks south along the strand.

Without footprints to guide her — they have either been washed away by the waves or blown away by the warm stiff breeze — April tracks William by instinct, trying to gauge which particular configuration of light, cloud, sea, sand, and grass, bird in flight, or driftwood might appeal to his eye. There's a certain laxity to his vision she recognizes from having posed for him when they first met. He likes to look at things that appear to have been flung down in front of him, attempting in his drawings to catch the world on the edge of motion. That's how he likes me, with my life in disarray, April thinks. But she can't know for sure. William has never found the words to express what he sees. He talks very little. In that respect, he is just the opposite of her father. And yet the hold he has on her reminds April all too much of the dead newsman who used to lead her along this same beach. It's not just words that can catch you. There are other ways. Mute infants. And dumb shows of love. She has another thought as she's walking, and it startles her. If her father were alive, they'd probably quarrel all the time.

"William?"

As though a hand had flicked the edge of a scarf in her face, the wind slaps her words back at her.

"Will?"

She looks down the beach toward the car, the family now no more than a dark blur on the dunes. To her left are the leaping waters of the gulf, ahead of her the sunny sky above Mexico. At her right, the dunes rise to the height of her chest. She climbs high enough to survey the leeward side of the island.

Here three men stand in a trough between the waves of sand, two of them poised with rods in their hands, their lines stretching beyond the range of dunes that edge the shore. The third man is William, hands at his sides, staring into the grass.

At first, she thinks the two men have gone mad, casting into the sand rather than into the ocean at their backs. Then she recalls the old custom of baiting hooks with savory bits of meat to attract coyotes, those wild scavengers with a bounty on their heads who made the dunes their home. Once, as a child, she had disobeyed her father and wandered away from the Christmas Day picnic, just as William has now, and watched as a lone angler hauled in a yipping, whimpering patchy-coated coyote, hooked through the jowl.

She doesn't wait to see it happen again. Poor William, she thinks, as she stumbles her way back among the dunes, recalling his empty hands: he had no intention of sketching anything. In her struggle this morning with her family, she hadn't even noticed that he never brought his materials along with him. A high-pitched shriek, but whether of beast or bird or woman or baby she cannot immediately determine, rises suddenly on the wind. Something catches in her throat, and she races along the shifting sand to answer a cry of distress.

Candace

'It's Caddy!' the librarian whispered. 'We must save her!'
Appendix to *The Sound and the Fury*

I

1

Hooray for Hollywood! The palms and sea mist, they knocked her for a loop! Flattening her hand against the front fender of the car, she tugged at her broken heel as if her touch alone might fix it. The driver, having deposited her worn valises onto the sidewalk in front of the hotel entrance stood sulking, nursing his hand, just a few paces behind her.

"Mis' Aitkins," the driver muttered.

"Goddman, you still here? I thought you'd be heading back for the Rockies by now..."

"I'm supposed to see you settled in..." Again, his voice trailed away, subsumed into the strangest sound, the murmur of the nearby ocean and the rattle of automobiles passing to and fro with a frequency known only in the wealthiest of districts.

"Settled in? You'd love to see me settled, and you'd love to settle in me..."

The driver punched the side of the car.

"Don't get so dramatic, Johnny-Bonny, you can't cure your cut and bleeding with a metal massage."

The driver might have said something else but she couldn't have heard it. A large open car roared past, spitting smoke and the shouts of its cheerful occupants. The driver leered at her, looking back long enough to make his passengers fear for their lives. And they screamed all the louder, some it appeared, in fright, others in amazement.

"How come I didn't get here sooner?" She addressed her question now to the rising spires of the exotic building some dozen yards away which bore the name *Nice Plaza*. Leafy plants formed a border separating the pavement from the grounds. Either she knew the answer or knew none was possible since she didn't pause to listen for any reply. "Goddman, I don't even know *how* I got here!" She turned and again addressed the sulking driver. "With you driving, Johnny-Bonny . . . "

A little fellow dressed in a sky-blue coat and cap came running up the path from the entrance.

"Good afternoon, Ma'am," he chirped, and smiled servilely.

"You have a shoemaker in your hotel?"

"A shoe repair service, Ma'am?"

"A shoe repair service, yes?"

"Why, yes, we do."

"Then pick up my bags and show me the way to it."

"Good-bye, *Madam*," said the sulking driver.

She did not look back. Somewhere around Sacramento he had pulled the car over and tried to kiss her and she had yanked off her shoe and hit him in the hand. That had calmed him down quite a bit, but now he was acting snarly again. I'd have given you rabies if I could have, she had told him, and if I could have I wouldn't have wasted a good heel on your hand. They had not spoken for the remainder of the trip, not even to exchange good mornings when she had emerged from the hotel in that town whatever it was called the day's drive north of where they now stood.

"Could you please mail this for me," she said to the bellhop, removing from her bag one of the letters she had written to occupy her time during the silent part of the drive. He accepted her request with a smile.

Hooray! She'd biffed and sneaked and slinked and scraped for the last decade. Sometimes she had followed men like dogs, sometimes men had followed her. But she'd never walked with as much smartness and stiff-necked strut as she did the twenty yards or so up the path—broken heel and all—to the entrance of the stucco castle by the sea.

Colors, shapes, a gush of people flowed around in the lobby. More palms, brittle-leaved and healthy, spread their limbs in welcome. Other trees unnameable to a Mississippian stretched to the balcony of the second floor where gentlemen in sport caps and steel spectacles looked down with great interest upon her arrival. If the hotel had a mind it would be thinking: who is this woman? what men will try to woo her? If the scene were in the movies as she imagined it could have been, the viewer would have all eyes focused on her flashy figure. But it was more like a ball at the Judge's house in French Lick, more like a stage play, most like a musical. The air glistened with the glint of silver candle holders, and dabs of color emanated from pots of fresh flowers on tables here and there about the lobby. Whirling about in the presence of, she might even call what she felt, despite her halting gait caused by her broken heel, a life as best she lived it.

"Chippy? Where are you, Chippy?"

A frail voice broke through the crowd's chatter.

"Chippy? Chipper?"

A mother had lost her child! Only God could make such accidents happen and still let you live...

"Chiiiipy?" Shrill now, her cry turned to purer pain.

Then up trotted a dog no bigger than a delta mosquito and it barked at her mistress' ankles until the woman, now smiling broadly, lifted the little beast in her arms.

"Ah, Chiiipy... Mam's is missed you where you been a dog too mischiefy..."

Candace felt her heart sputter, burst, and then something fell heavily through space, like a daredevil she once loved up in Memphis whose parachute failed him one Fourth of July.

"Boy!" she called to the bellhop when sighting him at last through the torn curtains of the palms. "You see if that driver of mine is still outside. Tell him I got to speak to him right away 'bout some bags I left in the car! And I want you to be sure my room looks out on the water!"

"The Ocean, ma'am?"

"*The* Ocean!"

2

... *Beautiful dreamer* ...

It was worth her last penny. The music shimmered in the air, the curtain dissolved into layers of light, thick and luscious you could cut them with a knife. On stage, a swing flew riderless through space, then picked up a woman at the far right and swung back and the woman faded away mysteriously into the rainbow mist of music.

... *wake unto me* ...

How many times she'd seen this show? Candace held her breath as the woman swung out once more over the orchestra pit, revealing garters, gauze pants, sly glances from her large harlequin eyes. She clenched her teeth, touched her knees together, took another breath.

"A dying art," sighed a bald man sitting next to her.

"I've done it and I'd do it again if they let me," she said, but the man had addressed his comment to another man on his right.

Two baggy-trousered comedians appeared near the lip of the stage.

"... said it was alright. So I took *two* bites!"

She thought of her room, its view of rough surf, hidden rocks. Soon she'd leave it. But not the ocean, never.

"Well what *is* so different about the carpenter's daughter?"

"Oh, you ought to see her *anvil* down the street!"

Her tower room protruded through the mist. She could see its turret windows. She fingered her purse.

"Pardon me." When she bumped knees with the bald man, he laughed so hard he sweated.

"My pleasure. Pardon me." He wiped his eyes with his coat sleeve. "You sat here last week, didn't you? I watched you from the other side of the aisle. You really enjoy this dying art."

"I used to be an entertainer myself."

"And where was that?"

"On the southern circuit."

"I know it well. Did you play the *Ruby* in—"

"*Who was that wife I saw you with last night?*"

"That's flattering of you to say."

"*That was no wife!*"

"Certainly, I could."

"*That was my lady!*"

"Why'n't you tell me your name so I don't feel out of place talking to you this way?"

3

Squatting in a stream bed
red tie

She woke up shivering. Stale cigar smoke filled the turret spaces, misted her windows.

4

She posted a letter and this is what she imagined: a clerk would pick it up and read the address; then he would place it in a special box for mail for that section of the country; minutes later another clerk would pick up the pile of mail accumulated there and tie them together for faster passage toward the south; then a train would speed them toward Memphis (?) or Little Rock (?) or New Orleans (?).

She watched through the slot but no one appeared. She turned away, smoked a cigarette, read a wanted poster. No one appeared.

"Excuse me," a voice came from behind her.

"I'm sorry," she said, standing aside so that a slender dark-haired woman her own age (or perhaps slightly older) could slide her letter into the slot.

"They don't come running to fetch them," she said.

"What's that?" The woman smiled. "You speaking to me, honey?"

"I said they don't bust their tails rushing to grab up the letters."

5

"That's enough. You sound like a nigger mammy at a funeral but you look terrific. We might have something for you coming up soon."

Candace smiled at the man as she slipped behind the wall of ladders and empty barrels. Her chest ached.

"How long they been keeping you down on the farm, honey?" asked the wardrobe lady when she turned the costume back. "You got a real nice future if you stay out of the light."

"What the hell you mean by that?"

"They do a lot with make-up but you stay out of the light."

Standing there before the mirror wearing nothing but high-heeled shoes and a kerchief, Candace wanted to punch the old woman in the face. But she resisted.

"I was more afraid about my voice."

"You should be. I heard you sing. But he likes 'em like you look so he don't tell the real truth."

"What's the real truth?"

"You're a lot like ten dozen others. But less pale, more lines."

Candace shivered, caught in a cold draft from the stage beyond the ladders.

"Will he use me?"

"God, will he!" the old wardrobe woman cackled.

6

One day Maeve followed her from the hotel. Candace visited a dress shop, her hairdresser, a tea shop, a palmist, and then the post office. In the post office, she wrote a letter and mailed it right there. Then she went to the Sisters of the Bleeding Wound Orphanage. Maeve waited for her outside for an hour and then gave up and went home.

7

Squatting in the stream bed

8

My country tis of thee
Sweet land of liberty
Of thee I sing...

She stood between two of the oldest girls, holding their frail hands tightly while the nun held up large photographs of famous places: The Lincoln Memorial...the Jefferson Memorial...the Washington Monument...

Your bodies are like these temples. Never forget that.

A photograph of New York City as seen from a ferry boat.

This land...

One of the little girls squeezed her hand.

"I got to go."

"Can't you hold out just a minute, darlin'!"

"I got to go."

"Well...if you got to go, you got to go."

"So do I," said the other little girl. One was white, the other swarthy. Each of them smiled alike, as though trained before the mirror at such matters.

"Well, kin I take you, honies? Show me the way."

"It's like Alice through the rabbit hole," said the darker girl.

"What's that?"

"It's a secret way. You're too big to come."

"I could try."

"All right," said the light-skinned girl. "Come along."

9

"Where'd you meet this one? In a post office?"

"I met him at the studio. He saw me once from a car."

"You're so lucky, Caddy. I meet bellboys and cops and you meet producers."

"We'll see what he can produce. I'm tired of vaudeville, I'm tired of running around looking for something I know I won't like when I get it! I'm tired of . . . everything I have to do. I once had a life!"

"Not much from what you told me about it."

"I'm a mother . . . "

"Are you drunk?"

"I am *not* drunk."

"Let me smell your . . . Candace Aitkins!"

"Oh, go'n Maeve, I'll crown you. It was just a little goofing with some of the ladies in the wardrobe department."

"What fluid they give you to drink while you was talking?"

"Told you I drink nothing. That's a habit I give up when I stopped living with my husband. And it's a good thing I did you know I was never one to hold my liquor."

"Candace, I'm worried about what you're doing to yourself . . . "

"Don't you worry 'cause I done most of it already."

"Yeah, honey, but the trouble may be you don't understand that even after you give yourself what you think you deserve there's a lot more to go on living after that. You figure you done everything you wanted to do and get everything by the time you're twenty-five that's swell. But what about the next forty years or so you got to live? People in the books, in the moving pictures, they end when the story ends but real people go on waking up every day after their tragedies happen and they have to make up their faces and eat their breakfast and catch a street car for work."

"I'm as real as all that. I do those things. I eat, I sleep everyday." Candace sank down onto the rug and stretched her arms above her head. "I'm so human in fact, Maeve, I think I'm going to be sick."

Maeve kneeled alongside her, stroked her forehead.

10

Candace lay on her back, felt him thought about pear blossoms a tree she'd never see

11

The ocean writhed on the horizon and now and again leaped as though it were in tune with the moon's pulse. Foam and moon glitter gathered at wave top when the surf rolled. A scent of salt and rich cigar smoke curled above her.

"What's this place called, Mister Herman?"

"It's just a beach."

"I like it." She stroked the back of his hand, aware of his thigh against hers.

"My house lies just down the way, dearie. Care to stroll in that direction?"

"And leave this big old car all by its lonesome on the beach?"

"We could drive then." His body twitched, as though he sensed something might roll in on the surf's rough curl. There was something odd about him; she could sense it but not say the name.

"Or stay right here."

"As you wish."

"I like you."

"Because I'm funny."

"You don't agree with me, do you?"

"I've always known I've been funny, Miss Compson."

"For Chris'. Mister Herman, please call me Caddy. That's what they called me back home." She rebelled against saying more. But her body went slack at the thought of all that. "Perhaps we *should* walk."

"Will you tell me about yourself, Caddy, if we do?"

"I'd tell you anyway, Mister Herman."

"And now you call me 'Herm.'"

"Herm . . . " She then told him only part of her story, but that was enough to make him gasp, sigh, and then, with the sound washed out by the waves, but because he was sitting so close to her with enough force to shake her as he shook, he wept. Lifting herself ever so slightly off the seat, she eased out a bubble whose sputter was so faint she only felt its gently dying vibrations beneath her panties as the ocean's growl drowned whatever noise it might have made before he heard it. "I shouldn't have said anything about my daughter . . . " Who opened the door next to her? She must have, and yet she did not recall the act.

"Come back, Candace," Herm called to her. He caught up with her, but not soon enough to keep her from soaking her dress in the high-blown spume from the breakers.

"I grew up in Coney Island and I know dangerous water when I see it," he murmured to her as he led her by the elbow back toward the car. "Once a little boy, a real young-un, from our very own block . . . "

She broke free and ran a few paces toward the blackness behind the car. Then she stopped, as though she found herself at the end of a taut leash, and she screamed: "You know dangerous water when you see it? You know dangerous water? I've been to hell in a washtub full of water and still don't know the difference between plain and complicated! I still don't know the difference! So come here, come closer, you dare? I dare you! Come closer and I'll show you what I mean. I wish I could show you what's like to be me and live like this, day in, day out, all these years that seem too brief and still fill up each day with so many hours I could run off into that world's washtub ocean and show my face no more—"

"You come home and wash your face, you'll be all right, then, you'll feel better."

She squirmed in his rough grip, he had a surprisingly strong grip for a man his size, but anyway she didn't want him to let her go and so she cursed only a short time longer and then let him subdue her.

"You caught me in the dark," she said. "You found me out."

"I saw you."

"You saw me? You saw the lines of it shooting out from me?"

"I make movies that have to show people those things. My movies make people laugh or cry depending on, if we know enough tricks, what we want from them, which means really what we think they want. There, there." He petted her as though she were the cat she never owned as a little girl. "You come home with me now, I'll make you happy. There, there . . . "

"Even if'n I don't wanna be?"

"There, there . . . "

12

Watching the pale fellow with the face as round as a full moon, she imagined that he didn't even come up to her breasts: Now what would he be like, she mused, waiting for him to reach the top of the ladder. Why he'd be like my big baby, all tender and moony and moany. That gave her a chill. She squirmed in her chair. Pay attention, she commanded herself.

The man fell backward off the ladder and she roared in laughter along with everyone else except for the sour little man in the golf cap behind the megaphone. Later he came over and introduced himself.

"I'm Frank," he said.

"And I'm earnest," she said.

"Save that for the vaudeville," he said, showing her that his sour expression was all an act itself. "You're Herm's friend, ain't you?"

"I'm a friend of the arts," she heard herself declare and thought she was as funny as the moon-faced man on the ladder. God, I don't know what I am till I find myself saying it.

"You ever do any vaudeville?"

"A lot," she lied.

"Where?"

"In . . . Memphis."

"You want a be in a moving picture?"

"Don't you think I'm a little too old for that?" she asked, feeling her voice go all girlish in spite of herself.

13

So hot in this room I could melt.
 Dear Mama
 Strips off a stocking.

I arrived here not too long ago
Another.
So damn hot.
Raises an arm. Sweat runs like a creek down a hillside.
Brother, it is hot!
Peels off panties.
This hotel cools me off. Never thought I'd see more sea than the gulf

Oh

Mama this ocean at evening time the colors of the sun settling like a liquid egg of flamish organe organe o-r-a-n-g-e over near the palms of beaches that stretch beneath the ocean toward Japan.

Summers at home, with dark squatting down on us so quick you'd think some scrappy child'd caught the bugger sun in a with a fishhook near its eye and yanked it down to bleed elsewhere over some other folk's horizons
Mama
I will write this if it kills me I am going to learn to express these things
Papa's health
Dresses for my beloved quickbeautied girl
Read a book with words strung together in it last week and have finally settled

brother!

overhead in oasis deseter film scratch that out

desert revue I hope to find a part in perhaps it will work out that I might work as an assistant to a movie producer who knows

"Thought you was getting dressed?"

"Too hot to do that yet."

"Why'n't you just go like that? Bound to give you a part."

"*You're* a bitch."

"You don't have to share my room with me, Miss Mississippi Moss or whatever you got down there."

"Down where?"

"Don't get touchy, love. I meant down there in Mississippi."

"Back East, you should say."

"Where I grew up, it was down below. If not beneath us."

"You know, Maeve, you are getting kind of snippy like. Keep it up and I will move out."

14

"And sedge a fadda nistic! Take that that and that!"

The large round moon slicked swiftly through the air and bits of cream scudded from its sides.

"Missed! Well, here a bell mad house! I'll just stick it right in there!" The fat man loped towards her, frightening her a little with his squeaky voice and the mad gleam in his eye. He loomed above her, fatter than taller but bigger than she. An illusion? That didn't matter.

"Oh, now, heavens!" She threw up her hands. "Could you do that to a little girl like—"

Muff! The creamy pie slugged into her mouth and her eyes stuck together. Slop, slippy lickity, it tasted awful and delicious at the same time. Whirling about, she could hear the fat man's breathing. Then he grabbed her breasts and hugged on for dear leer . . .

"Enuf!" came the director's cry somewhere outside her cream-sight. "This is the worst I've ever seen! Get the hell out of here, all of you! Everybody get ready for the second scene. Where's Herman? I got a bone to pick wid him!"

15

She used a typewriter now.
DEAr MAMA,
        YOU OUGHT TO SEE ME

16

The dream returned.

17

"Ladies and Gentleman, I would like to introduce to you my new business associate and beloved wife, Miss Candace Aitkins, for-merly of Indiana and Mississippi."

"To the new Mrs. Freed!'
"A toast!"
"Speech! speech!"
"I hope my vaudeville experience..."

18

squatting in a water

19

He threw her onto the bed and her slip rose up over her knees.
Without a sound, he tore away the cotton panties, leaving her naked
to his rough and probing fingers. Someone watching might have told
her that his unsheathed cock spewed sperm across her belly but all
she noticed was the cross dangling from his neck chain. He forced
her to touch her tongue to it. She nipped a piece of skin from his
shoulder and his outcry burst her eardrums. Blood ran down the
bedstead to the sea.

20

She went to a doctor and he gave her a powder to help her sleep.

21

        black
My father.
My brothers.
        My daughter
My mother.

22

I screwed him good that day.

23

She'd wear the fanciest dress that fifty bucks could buy. Her hair all golden in that summer sun the best cocks in town'd stand and crow for her attention. Music of ocean at her window, this vision dispersed. I am not she, she not me, or her us him at when. Useless wandering.

These damned headaches goin' to drive me out of my own brain if I can get away somehow! The wind whacks at my temples like it was a hurricane, I look around and the lightest weed ain't stirring but a frazzle . . .

"Your bodies are like temples . . ."

24

"I want you to turn out the light now, Candace. If you want to keep on writing, you can go to the study. You may have noticed we have a few extra rooms in this shit house . . ."

"I'd rather sit here with you, Herm."

"I have to be at the studio at five. Which is in exactly four hours. We've been drinking six hours with your friend Maeve and her low-class boyfriend. Need I say more?"

"So she likes bellhops. Chacun a son goût."

"And shacunt a son goo to you too Miss Assippi. I would you to turn out the light and come to bed."

"I'm sorry that my pleasures turn out to give you pain, Herm."

"That's a wonderful line, darling. You should write it down quickly before it melts. Except for two reasons. One, the stage is a dead form of entertainment, and two, people don't talk that way."

"I do. I always did, and I do now."

"You do, that's true. But if you heard that line on stage you wouldn't believe it. So it doesn't matter what's real or not but what you believe when you're in the audience. And I wouldn't believe it if it hit me in the face with all its curlycues and Southern drool. So turn out the light."

"Would you like *this*, Herm?"

"You're a temptress, another Vonda Vambling. But I have to be at the studio in three hours and fifty-seven minutes."

"Come out on the terrace a minute then and look at the ocean with me."

"Open the door. I'll listen from here."

"I want you to listen with me."

"What do you hear in that ocean, Candace? Mermaids? All I ever hear is crashing and gnashing. It reminds me of my gut."

"Same here, Herm. But I guess we got different insides."

"And outsides in case you think I don't have eyes. I see what you're showing me, honey. But I got to get to sleep."

"Perchance to dream . . . "

"That's a good line. You write that down."

"Don't be snide, honey."

"I'd rather be snide than sleepy. Good night, my little delta flower. Turn off the light."

"You'll say goodnight to all this?"

"You're the mermaid trying to lure me to the rocks. But I can't see through my eyelids so you can't lure me too far."

"Life is just one long joke to you, isn't it, Herm?"

"Life is the saddest thing I ever discovered I couldn't escape from, darling, so's I make movies to make people laugh a little and forget about it all."

"Why do I live here with you, Herm?"

"Because you like the terrace overlooking the beach . . . "

"What if I leap from that terrace, what'd you do then?"

"Leap? You'd jump. Please, don't use lines like that . . . not credible . . . Candace, I'm sinking fast . . . "

"Sink, you faggot kike. I'm going to throw myself off the terrace and make such a scene like you'd never believe but the whole world'll know —"

Faster than she thought he could move he threw aside the covers, leaped from the bed, crossed the space between them in one bound and slapped her so hard across the mouth that she staggered backward through the space between the open doors and only the waist-high railing kept her from falling. The light went out and she was left with the roar of the surf and her heart beating faster than she had ever felt before. Something in her life had changed and whether for better or for worse didn't matter since the sense of flux itself terrified her beyond her wildest imaginings.

25

Damuddy, can you hear me? Can you hear? I'm moving water. Turds in running stream. I climbed a tree and saw you lying there. From that time forward, I loved you.

26

"If you have dreams like that, you should see a reader. You never know what they could be trying to say to you."

"Maeve, I can't help but think I should come back and live with you. I'm so unhappy."

"Have another drink, Caddy. That'll make you feel better. Say, why'n't we trade places I'll go live in that big house of yours and you can have all my clients."

"You're joking, honey. I'd give anything to come back and live this life again. I just may do it."

"It's not so bad, is it? Why, see this necklace? A big producer over at Vita-Pix gave it to me last week. And you know what? I'm going to see that old friend of yours in Palm Springs *next* week. It's not so bad, is it?"

"No, not at all, Maeve. Herm's been wonderful to me but I just can't stand it any longer. He's... he's not normal, you know."

"What's he make you do? He make you do things with... you know, like that Frenchie we used to hear about over at the Wilshire?"

"He doesn't do anything but work and sleep. Course, he takes me to the best restaurants, God, we love to eat. He's let me write a script for a new movie they're making. But, God, I'm all written out and want to play a little and he's never there or when he is he can't do it."

"Caddy, honey," said Maeve, sliding next to her on the sofa. "How'd you like to write a part for me in that new movie of yours?"

"It's serious, Maeve," said Candace. "No pie throwing or that silliness."

Maeve gave Candace a squeeze and lay her head against her breast.

"Bet you could write something in for an old war horse like me?"

"Sure, I could, Maeve," said Candace, sliding her hand along Maeve's waist. "I think you'll like it. It's about a young southern girl who's abandoned by her boyfriend and then turned out of her family 'cause of that. She carries her baby to term and then leaves it at an orphanage..."

Maeve made a quiet assenting noise and nuzzled her cheek against Candace's breasts.

"Wonder who that could be about?"

"She's a wild, wild girl, smokes cigarettes, and drinks whiskey in places no girl her age's ever allowed into without some kind of special beau."

Maeve eased her hand inside Candace's bodice and raised her nipple with her touch.

"Herm says it's like nothing they've ever done before 'cause she's wild and free and all the goodie-goodies are goin' to be shocked by her but he thinks that we can do it if we just suggest things, you know, without showin' them directly."

She squirmed and gave Maeve a friendly squeeze. "Darlin', I can't talk when you're giving me the chills like that."

"Honey, I'm going to fix you another drink."

"Why'n't we smoke this reefer instead? One of the camera boys gave it to me, said it was the best in Hollywood."

"I'll try anything once."

"There's the difference 'tween you and me, honey. I just keep on counting."

II

Dear Mama,

Now we can call it two. You may be shocked at that, me writing about it the way I might be telling you about the score of a baseball game or the number of guests we had for tea, but that's the way I am and by now you ought to know. A daughter who's been married twice and divorced twice and quite a shame to her family. But not to herself. But if you're going to read any further in this letter and hear about what a beautiful place this is down here, a place you've never been but would love to hear about and perhaps someday soon your health and finances permitting even come down to visit then you will have to accept the fact that I came down here for that reason. So there's the only ugly thing that you'll find in this letter and I'm glad I said it and now I will tell you about all things bright and beautiful and gay and frolicky and the colors Mama the colors you have never seen them until you come down this way south of the border, the purple of the jacaranda just like home, the oranges of the flowers we never see even though we were nearly tropic, dark mountains that flash silver at you in the first light of morning, green so green it *defines* the color, Mama, and a sky that stretches so far around you when you stand on this central plain of the plateau of the state of Jalisco — none of those dirty old border towns for me, I'll tell you, I went deep south, Mama, south of south, our South, to this place which is nearly a thousand miles south of where you're sitting and reading this letter — Mama, so far south Jefferson is *north*!

Oh, Mama, I married a hick and then I married a Jew and I deserve to be here celebrating after a divorce. The first time, you remember I wrote to you about it, I mourned as though someone I knew well had died.

Well, I lost the train there, didn't I? And you know why? Because I was biting into a mango, and the juice rolled down my lips and over the bodice of a lovely white lace dress I had made for me the week I was waiting around for Herm's lawyer to finish up doing his business, which was mainly talking to people and paying bribes. You've never tasted a mango, I'll reckon, Mama, and let me describe it to you. The fruit is shaped like a sweet potato but the skin is greenish orange and smooth, and you've got to prick the skin with a knife or a fingernail but not so deeply that you can't just lift up a flap of skin and peel it back in strips. The edible part is pulpy, overbrimming with juices, and you've got to bite quick and suck the meat into your mouth and savor it there. Try to nibble at it and you'll end up the way I did, with a soiled bodice and a need for a napkin and a bowl of water.

The waiter, a dandy little boy about fourteen, slender, dark, and somewhat undernourished, quite unlike the way our brother looked at that age, muscley, even mealy-muscley looking, Mama, if you know what I mean, as though somebody had sprayed his arms with grit you could see the shape of underneath the bulgy skin, this waiter just helped me clean myself up. I can't tell you how much help the men down here offer me. Ha, Mama, that was a joke. They're impolite, shall we say, in the extreme, and I have to every now and then give them a smack the way you do mosquitoes back home at night after the lights go down. They are plain fresh and nasty. Primitive is what an English friend I have made the acquaintance of at a pretty whitish-colored lake called Chapala calls them. He says that they are not like niggers but that they are more like Indians, a different race, and that their art and culture as he calls it is a grade above the Africans who made their best art three thousand years ago and the Egyptians who made their best art four and five thousand years ago.

The other day, just on the day I met this man (who is travelling with his overweight German wife who has a sharp tongue and is always making eyes at the waiters even if they are fourteen, Mama, I must tell the truth), we took a rickety bus ride for nearly two hours to the other side of the lake and then we discovered that the bus didn't go back to our hotel and we had to rent a boat and get ourselves rowed for miles back to the other side. A great rainstorm came up out of the west and we had to row to the nearest island which the owner of the little bar in the shack on the center of it said was called Scorpion Island. Because of the shape? my English friend asked. Because of the scorpions, the bartender said back to him, and the Englishman nearly jumped out of his shoes. LOOK OUT for them! he shouted to his wife, and to me, and he stood up on the little picnic table the bar owner had set up for people to sip their beers at, and he wouldn't come down for nearly ten minutes after the bartender explained in broken English that he was only making a joke, that it was the shape of the island. Oh, Mama, we had a good time as good as any time I'd had since you and I went to French Lick together that summer what seems such a long time ago . . . I laughed so hard myself I had to pee, and so I went around to the back of the only trees nearby on this tiny place (Oh, Mama, will I ever send this dirty letter to you or shall I rub out these nasty lines with mango juice or ink) and there I was with my then quite new white dress raised up over my knees, me squatting there, my little new white undies slid down to my ankles, and just as I was feeling on the verge of peeing I saw — yes, you guessed it, if you're reading this letter Mama, you guessed it, a creepy crawly scorpion tiny as my little finger and looking more monstrous than a dinosaur. And you know what I did, Mama? So scared and all as I was? I watched him crawl toward me as though I was the London Bridge or a giant redwood and then when he was under me and God knows what he was about to do then crawl on or sting me in the place of places when he was under me yes I gushed down on him the way the heavens gushed down on us. May the Scorpion God have mercy on Its Soul!

Dear Maeve,
    I am disconsulate.

Dear Herm,
    Your deelightful check arrived and I thank you my ex and my why. It is just simply so beautiful here that I'm not sure just how much longer I can stand it. Isn't that queer? Sullied — is that the word? — as I am by my past experiences, even the beautiful shapes and shades of this land

Dear Maeve,
    Mexico is a place for us bad-uns. I have had the naughtiest of naughties and all of it to the tune of the strings and fat bass fiddles crossed with guitars they call mariachees. Picture a lake the color of fresh cream with not a cloud in the sky to reflect on its surface. Plunk down next to it green mountains and a hotel or hacienda here or there with only the wind off the water to tell their inhabitants that a boat may be approaching from the other shore. In early morning, all is still. By noon, the servants have awakened and clean houses, patios, beaches, whole skyfronts with their funny brooms they call trapeadors or "husbands" because they sling them around with such glee but never seem to get much done with them. We take a wee drink or two at lunch and by late afternoon we sway to music not yet

begun to be played, the chirpy, brassy, punchy, twangy mariachee. Ee-ee!

Mostly I drink and take a bite to eat with the British couple (actually he's British and she's German) who've taken such a liking to me. I will tell you about him in a moment, poor dear that he is. But I ought to say something about what happened to the other

You see

I tried early mass at the tiny cathedral near the lakeside. It has a small altar of simple silver service, and a dark Indian lady and I were the only creatures kneeling. I didn't know exactly what to do.

Dear Lord,

I feel as though I were a creature in a story, my fate as far out of my hands as the clouds drifting off the shore of Scorpion Island. I have talked to friends about this. Some say that we all feel this way as if to dismiss it. Others say, yes, they have had the same feeling but the only thing to do is laugh it away. Lord, I can no longer laugh. Once, I could. Once, kneeling in a stream bed home, I felt the surging waters clean me free of filth. But Lord this pain no longer leaves. It is with me day and night, day or night, night or morning. Sweet and pungent orders odors no longer please me. The taste of all your good things leaves my mouth bitter. I am a slut and a whore and all terrible monstrosities of woman being. I have allowed men to touch me all over, and to pierce me all lover, and to saturate me all over, and to torture me all over, and taste me all over, and to show me all over, and Lord I no longer no which is myself, my own parts, and which are the parts of the world. Lord, if you told me even this pain that pierces down into the root of me, as though a sliver of sharpest wood had pierced me, were nothing but words on a page that would only increase the pain. Lord, if you told me that I had no being except what others thought of me that would only deepen the terrible loneliness I feel. Lord, if you told me that my dear dead father and my sick mother, and my dear, and dead, and damned brothers, mad and maimed by their own hands or by others each of them, if you told me that all of us or any of us had no being except what you told me that would only turn the screw tighter, twist the vine tighter around that part of me, how can I use any single word to describe it, that part of me, is it my heart, my soul, my spirit, my feeling, my nerves, my womb, my liver, my spine, my brain, my tongue, Lord, I have let men put themselves into me in the hope that would make the hell go away. And it did not. Lord, I have let men put other men into me in the hope that it would make the hell go away. And it did not. Lord, Lord, I have let other women put things inside of me in the hope that the hell would go away. And it stayed. Lord, I have let men and women Lord you have seen it I cannot say it but the hell stayed with me. Why did I get sent to hell before I died, Lord? Does that mean that I can go to heaven when I die because I am already in hell? Dear Lord, God, creator of the scorpion, have mercy on me.

Dear Maeve,

Have you ever tasted a mango? a papaya? a guava? The wonderful fruits they have here ain't no joke, darling, at all. Last night a dark devilish looking Mexican in a tuxedo took me for a carriage ride around the wonderful city of Guadalajara, and I ate mangos and threw the seeds out of the carriage and dark Indian boys rushed to catch the seeds because of the magical powers I must have put into them.

Dear Herm,

The check arrived and I am so grateful. Did you know what a wonderful time I could have here when you suggested that we do it this way? You are a wonderful person yourself to have suggested this to old me.

How is the picture going I have tried to read about it in the Los Angeles paper that drifts down here every now and then but find no news about it. Is Vonda still going to be the lead? And that deep voiced old cracker from near my old home town, what's his name?

Dear Mama,

I am having a fine time here, squired about as I am by every respectable tourist in sight. You would love this place except you can't drink the water. Perhaps some time I will come back up home and tell you face to face about what a good thing has happened to me.

How is She? You hardly ever say more than a few words about her when you write at all. I know how it is when you're ailing, but you must as a mother know how much the simplest phrases mean to me. Do you think you could get a picture taken? I would love that so much. Separated from her, I feel like part of my body itself has been taken from me. You do know yourself, Mama, what I mean.

Dear Lover,

You have gone back to Italy in such a huff that I don't even know what or why I'm writing this to you. But I did want to tell you that I miss your talk terribly, and that I have since you left gotten so tan myself that you might mistake me for a native. But the main thing I wanted to write to you about is my internal conversion and the things that it is changing in the outside part of my life. That night when we walked all the way to Ajijic and back and you told me about your writing and your own family and your illnesses and your special reasons for wanting me to come with you, I never could put in to words the feelings that I had then building up inside of me like rain clouds on the mountains in Michoacan. When you touched my hand with the back of yours, something electric went charging through me, and—remember!!—I fell back against the palm and you caught me, and you said that you had never known a woman whose voice in any language magnetized you as much as my own. You talked about my accent, and I was so surprised whenever anyone mentions that I never heard it I am surprised and tickled by it. You held my arm so tight I could feel the blood damming up at my shoulder and in my throat. I told you that I knew what you wanted. You said I didn't. I told you that I did. But first I had to ask you. I had to ask you, what does my life mean? I have tried love, and I have tried marriage, and I have tried love without marriage, and I have tried crimes and I have tried praying, I have tried smoking marijuana and drinking alcohol and eating the button of the peyote cactus, I have tried being a mother, I have tried, but it is so hard over this distance . . . Last night I tried to kill myself by walking into the lake and I could not go all the way. Does that surprise you? You knew I was that kind of person or you would not have held my arm so tight. Only men with serious intentions hold a woman's arm that way. Didn't you know our custom here? Calm, you said, and wait for the rhythm to come upon you. Calm, you said, and let the thing flow through you and out again into the soil. Christ, I told you all those things about me, all those things I never have spoken to anyone about, not even my two husbands. Calm, I am calm . . . I had waded out into the lake up to my waist. That gentle tide that you noticed for us the other day at the waterside lapped at my bosoms. Why, I might have been stepping into a bath the water seemed so warm. And then I remembered your words, and calm kept me steady, living, and I thought to myself, why, how can you do this, Caddy, your story's not over yet! And I laughed to myself, and I remembered your words, calm, and how your wife's eyes glistened when you kissed my hand at the casino, and how the mariachee band played all night, and I thought I was drowning in air, I didn't need water, because at that moment a thunderbolt slapped against the mountains on the Michoacan shore, and the music of the band drifted over the waters from the Casino, and I felt nothing less than just one big silly at the thought that I could kill myself when my story had not yet ended. I missed your accent all of a sudden, and the odd taste of your mouth when you kissed me under that palm tree. Can you really tell whether it's male or female from the smell of it?

How could that be? I waded back to shore, thinking that I must live on long enough to ask you that trick. Does a female palm tree have the monthlies? Does a male palm tree stand erect at the sight of a lady palm? Can you read your lady's palm when you're erect? Oh, isn't that a nasty thing for a lady to write when she knows a man only just a short time! Lover, I know this sounds perfectly insane but I must see you again soon, and since I have the cash ready for my ticket I'm going to buy a boat ticket as soon as I reach Veracruz, and sail for Europe. Will you stand still in your little house as you described it to me so lovely until my arrival? Will your wife hate me for writing this if she sees this? You're the only man who has ever made me think that I might want to live again with someone. I'm not like those silly young things — I'm just not young no more — you read about in novels and so I won't follow you to the ends of the earth. But I'll come, I'm coming, I'm already on my way, as you read this, to Italy. Ah, E-Tahl-Ya! as you shouted it. That night when the music drifted out upon the waters and you played me . . . I've never written anything like this before and I certainly don't expect to ever read it from someone else's hand — when you showed me what you needed and that was what I needed to . . . I've just heard a rumor that two Americans died on the road to Guadalajara, killed by bandits while riding in their motor car.

III

So I, who had never had a sister and was fated to lose my daughter,
set out to make myself a beautiful and tragic little girl. I returned to
Memphis in a state of shock so deep and profoundly disruptive of
the normal responses to the world that I did not know how disturbed I was until I was nearly well again.

Gone.

She was gone, when I arrived that April afternoon, and so I did
everything within my power to absent myself from felicity a while.
Compared to the life I took up on Beale Street and Yahnahmee and
Gayoso, pain was the gift of beings who had once had pleasures to
compare it to.

Gone. Disappeared. Vanished. (   ) Years spilled from my
life, like milk from an overturned pitcher.

'28, '29, '30. '31, '32, '33. I hear these were hard years for
Yankees, but where I sprawled most of it didn't mean all that much
to me. You with your European disposition ought to know something about what I mean when I say that. I knew and I didn't, I cared
and I didn't care, I was there and yet at the same time I was absent. I
was the impression absence leaves when it's getting gone from a
place where it's never been before and never will be.

I myself had known what disappearing meant ever since the day I
departed for Memphis in Herbert's fine car, my belly filled with the
seed of that child who would grow to disappear on the day that I
returned full circle from the west to the place I departed from.
Herbert, my husband-to-be, was driving while I sat suffering the
pains and pangs and shakes and trembles of a separation I never
willed but found myself innured to. Jefferson faded away into the
greenery behind us and ahead lay Eudora, a town not on the direct
route to Memphis but through which we rolled, just as splendid as if
we'd planned it, because Herbert, in his excitement had taken a
wrong turn.

Herbert, I said, I need a cool drink real bad. I was perspiring, I'll tell you, and not just because of the extra weight I had been carrying those last few weeks but because of the ordeal of the farewells. Or nonfarewells, since no one but mother came to see me climb into that car and depart, Papa and Jason being of one mind about my condition, and Quentin being... being... just a moment... I'm sorry, Doctor...

Now, I says, I need that soda pop.

Honey, I want to reach Memphis by dark, says Herbert. I got a real nice dinner planned for us at the hotel restaurant.

Which hotel? I asked.

He told me, and secretly I gave a cheer. It was the biggest and best, but I wasn't going to have that hotel and miss my drink so I told him that I would die and never reach that hotel and that room and that dinner he had his heart set on if I didn't have a drink of soda pop, and then I just leaned over and lay my head against his shoulder and let my hand drop into his lap and he gave a yelp like a pup with his nose caught in a doorway and nearly drove off the road into the porch of the country store just on the outskirts of Eudora. He never gave me any more trouble after that. That night he let me do what I liked and never asked more than once for me to do for him things that I told him I'd never do and that was that.

Gone. I left him alone in the room that night, walking by myself for about an hour through strange Memphis streets, and finding myself taunted and tempted but not attacked by men with obvious intentions. I wanted to stay with him but found I could not. He had been so handsome in his white suit at French Lick that for months after he courted me I couldn't think of him in any way but that. But in the hotel room, with his white suit on the bed and his turkey neck hanging limply between his balding knees he was a sight to behold. For a few minutes. And then flee from, as I did.

Gone. Whatever feeling I had for him and for the life that we would make together left me almost as quick as we ourselves packed my things into the shiny new automobile and left the home county.

Gone. Like the years that flowed from my life after I returned to Memphis.

Like Herbert himself.

He never forgave me for that night. I know that for a fact, because he wrote to me now and then letters that always turned back to that one evening, and how much it hurt him to discover my true nature. Doctor, is this what this talk's supposed to do? bring back those words, those moments when the pain came on so strongly that I want to forget about them forever but can't? *Gone*. But he wrote before he died the other month of a heart attack that he still remembered the way I looked at him after we got undressed. I was a bit silly from the champagne but from the look in *his* eye he was stone sober and not about to think of anything else but what he wanted to happen next.

You hep me off with this dress now Herbert, I teased him, seeing him standing there in his underdrawers. He reminded me of Daddy on nights when he came upstairs so drunk he forgot that we could see him if he left his bedroom door open too wide. I'm rambling. I should tell you what happened then. You're right, this ain't no story this is my life and I do want things to get better, 'though I know better than you do that they can always take a turn for the worse. And then another turn. Like the one we took to Eudora instead of continuing on straight north toward Memphis.

You hep me off with this dress. Like that, that's right. God, I kissed him until I thought my lips were going to bleed, that's right. And then I guided his hands here I don't mind shame no longer applies in my life I've seen the worst turns downward toward Hell and its countryside, which are located somewhere northwest of Memphis but you can't find them on the map. So I stepped out of my dress and he stepped out of his drawers and we were playing statue of a nude to each other's gazes when it came to me that I was truly thirsty and I asked him to fetch me another cool drink. He laughed and took me in his arms but I told him that nothing was going to happen until I had that cool drink and so he went into the bathroom and ran the tap and filled me a glass of water and I told him that wasn't cool enough I wanted a real drink and so he went into his suitcase and came out with a bottle of whiskey and I told him I wanted soda pop and he called me a goose and I told him I wasn't kidding and that if he didn't get it for me that I'd go out and fetch it myself. Well, me. You should have seen his face.

Candace, he said. I'm taking you away to marry you and give your child a father.

My child has a father, I said. Just 'cause it ain't you don't give you reason to be so mean to me. I want a soda pop.

Candace, you get over here, he said.

No!

Candace, you step over here or I'll come spank you.

No! You get that soda pop and you can do what you like but you get nothing until then.

His mouth turned sour-like, and he suddenly seemed to know that if I didn't want him to strip his shoes and socks off real quick that I must think he ought to cover himself up instead. I am going to marry you, I'm taking you away from the troubles you got at home because you lived so badly, I'm going to give you a house all your own big enough to keep you happy and I'm going to make your brother a treasurer of a company and you tell me you won't do nothing for me until I fetch you some soda pop?

Thass right.

You're talking like a nigger, he said. Stop that nigger talk and you come here.

Don' cho lahk me to tawk lahk dis here, Hehbet, spooning on nigger like chocolate onto a ice cream sundae. Whass wrong, hon-ee? You don't want to held yo-sef in check til you gets de sodee pop for Mis' Candace?

You stop that and come on over here.

No! I stamped my foot and stood my ground. You fetch me that pop.

You talking like you're drunk.

I ain't drunk now, you should hear me talk when I'm drunk, I don't need to be drunk to talk this way 'cause I watch my father and mother talk like this all my life. Now you go and fetch me that pop, Herbert, or you just ain't going to use that thing of yours tonight.

He blushed, looked down quick at it, and laughed.

God, you're a nasty bit, aren't you? I didn't know how nasty you were when I proposed to you.

I felt my belly, real casual-like. It felt good and taut and smooth, as though nothing was inside it but the thought of what I was thinking about in my head. Nothing alive that is, just thoughts positive and beautiful. Nothing at all to do with life.

Hell with the soda pop, Herbert, I said. I was just testing you to see how loyal you were to me your new little wife. And you just failed. I'm going home.

He was furious all of a sudden, now he realized I was playing games.

You're not going any further than that bed there, he said.

Ooooo! Herbert, I cooed, you're talking tough enough for me to feel real frightened. And I don't know what I'd do if I got scared. I pretended to look around for a way out.

You just get right over there, he said, advancing toward me. You just talked yourself into a real pretty pickle.

You got the pickle, Herbert honey, 'cept it ain't so pretty. Except like we say, pretty ugly.

God, you are a foul mouthed little thing you are, he said. I didn't know this much about you when I said I'd do all those things for you. You think I ought to do them now?

Herbert, I said, rushing to the window. I'm going to jump out on the fire escape and scream for help if you lay a hand on me.

No, you won't. You're my wife.

Not yet. I tried to open the window but it was locked.

Don't you do that. We're getting married tomorrow so you might as well be now.

If you can catch me we will, I said, unfastening the window lock and reaching up to pull the window open.

Don't you, hey!

Help! I shouted out into the street. No one looked up. Help, Papa!

Stop that. He grabbed my wrists and tried to wrestle me away from the window.

Help me, Papa Papa, help!

Now someone called up to the window, hey, what's going on up there?

Man and wife! Herbert called down, holding me by the wrist.

Rape! I screamed.

Hey, hey, you, you, shouts drifted up from the street.

Goddamn you, bitch, he said, twirling me about as though he was trying out a new dance step. Doctor . . . he was all swolled up down there, his pretty pickle, and the lights went out, I remember, though the window stayed open the entire time, and I let him push me over to the bed, and he did a few things to me, and then just as I had to decide what I wanted to do we heard a lot of feet running about in the hall, and loud voices, but though people came racing by our door no one actually knocked on it. Herbert was sweating, God, he was, and it was running down on to me since by now he was hovering over me like a old bear of the woods. His body was smooth and mostly hairless, but he had a funny way of sniffling that made me want to giggle as though he had a lot of hair and was tickling me with it. Then, just like the Catholics do sometimes, I heard a voice, it was a voice from inside me, crying, Mama, I'm alive, you be careful, be tender with the load you're carrying, you know who it is, and Doctor, as though it were for the twenty-ninth, instead of the fourth or fifth time I rolled over gently on my side and helped him in the sideways style so that my baby would not have to bear the weight of a man was not her father.

Poor Herbert! You ever been in Memphis when the lights went out? You never been any place in our country! You never been in the south, you never knew what it was like in a city like Memphis when the sun went down and all the country people go into hiding, just as Herbert was having us do, and all the city people (and southern city folk are strange, let me tell you), all the high divers come out and do their stuff on the dark. You know what we do? We take a long drink of some sweet tasting whiskey the way a diver takes a deep breath and then we plunge in over our heads into black light in dark alleys where you can wiggle your behind to your soul's contempt and never no one know the difference between penitence and penny toss 'cause it's always too dark to see. Why it's a sea so black and awful that the man who hears you cry rape one moment and rushes to your rescue will grab you from behind the next.

These boys out in the country they'll just grab hold of you. That's how they live, how they love to live. And you get one of these country lovers in the city and he'll do just about anything because he doesn't know how to act. He's a fish out of water. Fish. A real varmit, I mean, collecting the injuries of others as though they were cash in his bank account and he was counting the interest. And what the women do comes out of your case books too, what they do in the City of Dreadful Night. That's a title of a poem my dear dead brother sent me in a letter. I have the letter with me. I want to read it to you before I go.

Going, going. I left Herbert in the room and I descended into what some of my family thought I was from the beginning and into what others thought I was driven by my element to become. I took my time walking to the stairs, but Herbert didn't bother to call after me. He knew I wouldn't come back. I wanted him to call out to me, I'll admit, but I didn't want to come back. I didn't even want to look back not because I was afraid I'd turn into a pillar of salt because I was heading down the stairs towards rather than away from the cities of the plain—how my brother helped me to talk! I have to admit, since he wrote me that long letter, here, you see, I still carry it with me, since I am the recipient of letters rarely and the writer of many I carry it with me as a token of his love for me, and I write letters as the true act of love for my departed daughter who now has disappeared from the face of the earth as though an autumn tornado picked her up and carried her away into some never-never land that you might see in a movie made by some imaginative producer with a lot of cash and very few guts, my childish Herm maybe, I was descending the stairs and he did not call out, or if he did I didn't hear him, and by the time I reached the street three men had approached me. Dutiful dark inhabitants of the lobby of twilight, they leaped from their seats to catch me before I went out the door and into the street fearing that some infectious whim might strike me and prevent my return to their hotel where they made it their businessess to keep track of all the available women. Guided by one of them, the first one to reach me, (and that was all that mattered), I went to a cafe, drank my fill of whiskey, and allowed him to consider all of the possibilities which might have brought a girl as young as I was then to such a pass. Though I was going, I was not yet gone (and won't be until I finish my story) since what I realized just before deciding to come and speak to you, if only this once, was how long I had let others determine my ways and how little I had told about myself, and how small a part of my own life I had actually created myself, and for good or for evil or for both or neither (for if God made me this way, if anything could plan a mind such as mine, and feelings such as mine, and a life such as mine, then all things are possible).

Where you headed when I saw you? this tall slim jim with a cowboy tie and a glassy head of dark hair asks me.

To hell in a handbasket. Want to come along?

Where'd you learn to talk like that? You go up the university or something?

Don't need to do that, I said. My brother, he says, we're going to hell just fine without all of us getting our education.

Who's your brother, what's his name?

Jason.

I know him?

If you do, you're a bastard like him and I don't want to drink your money.

Well I don't know him. But I sure do like to know you. What's your name?

Besides.

That's right?

That's my name. Its a funny name but it's mine. Besides.

Besides what. Shit. You want another drink. It makes you into a real comedy star. You ought to drink more milk though, besides, because you're looking mighty skinny for a girl wants to attract real men.

Feel this, I say, taking his hand by the wrist and touching it to my belly. This going to require a lot of milk.

God, you are drunk.

Besides.

Drunk besides!

What do you call this place?

Ted Mooney's.

And this town?

Memphis, don't you know it's Memphis?

I don't know much but I know you got to give this town another name if I'm going to talk to you for more than one second more. I turned to the man at the left of me at the bar and he didn't seem surprised that he wanted to talk more to me. I was putting his hand on my belly when Cowboy Tie turned me around.

Hot City! he exclaims.

Hot damn! I scream back at him.

What you doing to this pretty thing? asks the man on the left of me. You fixing to fuck up her life?

You keep out her life, Bean Dog, says Cowboy Tie.

Or what? says Bean Dog.

Or I'll slice you up and feed you to nigger pups for breakfast.

Haw! haw! what the hell's a nigger pup? O! you mean what you and your family raise in your backyard and call them roses? Haw!

You stand behind me here, says Cowboy Tie to me, and with one motion which includes treating me rather tender-like since he knows I am going to be a mother and treating the situation rather seriously he swings me behind him and steps up to face Bean Dog. Except that Bean Dog isn't there. A knife is. And Cowboy Tie squints hard as the knife sweeps past his face.

Blood gushed across the bar, and I fainted.

When I awoke it was a lady standing over me, and no men in sight.

How'd you come here? she asks. She's about fifty, with lines that run rouge like water in irrigation ditches. Her dress is about as old as she is, least the style makes me think so. And she smells of outlandish perfume, Eau de Ham Sandwich or some such scent, until I realize that it's me I smell.

I don't know, I say squeezing or trying to squeeze up into a ball. I'm tired, sick to godman, I want to go home. Herbert? Where's Herbert? I ask her. I'm feeling just awful, like a bitty baby done done it in her pants and wants a Mama.

You wait here, I'll help you, she says. Temple?

I thought I was in some church.

Come help this girl clean herself up.

Yes, ma'am.

A younger woman brought me clean clothes. But they were a strange style and I told her I couldn't wear them.

You'll wear them, she says in a voice I didn't dare challenge.

How'd you get here? the girl dressing me asks.

I don't know, I said. I described the fight and all that and she says, oh. That's all.

You tell me the name of your hotel, the old lady says when she comes back into the room. I could hear laughing and piano music coming from somewhere on the same floor. I told her where we are staying and she laughs and says it ain't all that far from here. And she takes me by the hand and leads me out of the room, down a long flight of stairs, the piano music growing louder as we descend, and finally to a large green door leading, I correctly figured, to the street. I wish I could have stayed inside a while longer. The laughing and the music called out to me. I looked at the greenness of the outer door, my stomach felt awful and I wanted to sleep. I'll take you part way home, says the old lady, and we leave the house and walk a few blocks toward what became the center of the city and then she left me only a couple of yards from the hotel door.

This time was Herbert was gone. The room was locked, no one answered my knock, and when I went back down to the lobby to ask for the key the man at the desk told me that my husband had checked out. I cried all of a sudden, tears running down my cheeks like in a big home-style rainstorm. I pounded the desk top with my fists. The clerk tried to calm me down but I couldn't stop wailing. Then of a sudden across the lobby my name gets called.

Who's that? I spin around.

Lean long-faced man chewing on a pipe, newspaper across his knees.

He went up to Indiana, you got to follow him, this man says.

Damn if I do.

And if you don't, he says, flicking his eyes across me so friendly-like that I figured he didn't want me in any danger.

He give you the message? I inquire, still standing at the desk. I'm afraid to get too close to him so I won't be disappointed when I discover that his interest in me turns out to be like all the others in this state.

The man shrugs, which I take to mean, of course.

Your bag, Missus, says the clerk just then, sliding my only suitcase across the top of the desk. I asked him to hold it for a minute more, went to use the powder room on the ground floor, counted my money, and came back out to find the man with the pipe had disappeared, and my suitcase standing by the potted palm just at the door. Without looking back, I picked it up and hiked out the door to the bus station and caught the first bus to Indianapolis.

Herbert wasn't too happy to see me.

I thought you'd go back home, he said, standing in the living room of his folks' house, the place where he first told me how much he wanted to marry me.

Back there? I laughed as I unpacked. Your jokes just kill me, I said. Now I want to take a hot bath. It's not good for a woman in my condition to get so tired out.

I heard him arguing with his folks while I was running water in the tub. That argument didn't end until three months later when I left for good.

I don't know that I can explain just by talking to you. Gone, gone, gone, is the way it keeps saying over and over in my head, as what I felt and where I went and how I must have appeared to other people. I returned to Memphis, had my baby, gave it home, watched my father buried. I took up the theatre as a profession, which allowed me from time to time to return to the state. I watched my baby as she grew from nothing to a full-sized girl — there's many things involved in this that can't be said now or perhaps even ever. I thought for a time that I would be an actress who could make these bad feelings come out in my work but that didn't seem to mean much after a while I gave up on that and settled down to trying to stay alive minute by hour by day by month by year after year after year. Up to Denver; down to Salt Lake City; up to Omaha; down to Houston; over to Albuquerque; east to St. Louis; and then to the west. Doctor, I have travelled. So much since that time it has been hard for me to give myself time to think and study the parts of my life that hurt me the most the parts that I need to study so I can make the present good for me, the past is never past for me it is always present my mind sometimes seems to me like the grand opera house I played in so large the casts of three grand events performed in it at the same time and I was in the audience sitting near the rear, listening, nodding, praying, crying, laughing, oh, always with a sense of humor, waiting for the rehearsal to end. The last act means only another run-through from the beginning. The music. The lights. The jokes. The tintinabulation of the cymbals of the belles ...

Oh, there's story after story to tell. The night would have to stop disappearing to the other side of the world before I could finish. Up in Salt Lake, a driver, two months on the run with the proceeds of ...

or, There was once this man opened up a little theatre in a small town in the Northwest thought he could hire a troupe of ...

or, That in Aleppo once ...

or, Now Benson was a high shade of yellow and sported a mind like a fancy new car. And when we left for the I'll tell you about Herm at least. He was the best of a weak lot. Which speaks well for none of them; but not poorly for him. All of them, many things to say about the

Nights in Albuquerque hang in the high part of the sky, like the stars. You try to catch their passage but you fail ...

Three miles west of the edge of a small town near the northeast
pocket of . . .

Here is a woman. Do you know her? She has come a . . .

Two men could be seen walking along a stretch of gravel path . . .

It was in the year 1920 on a quiet April day

Inside the bar, the noises of the crowd subsided

. . . My father gave me a piece of advice . . .

Gifford married Karen on June 6, 196

"Number, please," said the operator

I could say anything, I could say carry me along taddy like you
done through the toy fair and what difference would it make. There
is no question about what will happen next, no question whatsoever
and because there is no question there need be no reason. No, I
don't think that I'll take my own life. We have in my family a
number of things that we have already accomplished, one of them
being suicide, the other being idiocy, the next being alcoholism, the
other being miserliness, and, godman, you might think that that was
enough to boast about but then you will have to add to the list,
which tacks on a number of venal sins, several mortal sins —
sometime I'll tell you how Clarsworth and I raised the money for the
vaudeville troupe — sometime — social disgraces, iniquities, as Dis
Dilsey we used to call her our Mama used to call what we did to each
other, dis dat and d'other, a barnfull of just plain disgusting behavior down to and including the night when Jason came bursting into
my room and caught me sitting with my legs up on the table and I
wasn't wearing any pants and he caught a look at me and started
shouting and jumping up and down and screaming so loud you'd
think it had a flashing-neon eye winking at him . . .

Now you have said nothing to me but that you think that I want to
make my life a living Hell . . .

Now you have asked me to write down for you what I can
remember about my past

Which to me is like a declaration of undependance from the
present which is fine with me since the moment I'm living in gives
me pain why not live in the past.

And so I thought that I would copy out for you part of a letter
which

(I'm stopping everything now because I just remember sitting on a
swing with the first man to put his finger inside me, is that the kind
of thing you need to hear)

part of this letter which my brother a educated boy sent to me
from college the one who killed himself

"*Noi siam ventui al luogo ov'io t'ho detto/ che tu vedrai le genti dolorose,/ ch'hanno perduto il ben dello intelletto.*"

Dear Candace,

I am speaking to you across all these miles and thinking how much I would like to hear the sound of your voice, hear you laugh. Here he quotes a lot of poetry which I cannot remember. And goes on. I raised that shade and looked out over the mountains of home, and saw that nigger on a mule as big as a rabbit, a sign, a landmark . . . I heard a bell of pure reverberation and it called me back to myself and I knew that purity lay beneath the water, was the water itself, remember the time in the stream bed how I could ever forget when we baptized each other with our own noneternal self-affection, and you said that you would run away and you ran.

I returned to Memphis once more before leaving behind forever that place where I couldn't live and yet couldn't live without. I knew how I felt about it because I made an abortive trip to Europe just after returning there as I said I did as I described to you the next to the last time when I found her gone, my mother ill, my family mostly dead and the ones left alive better off dead or ought to be dead and my husbands dead and I went to Italy to visit friends and they had died or gone away and only their empty house was there to greet me. And I left the doorstep of that house in Italy and turned right around and returned to Memphis because I knew in that moment when I didn't walk in the door of that villa because there was no one left to greet me there I knew then where she was. Yes.

Forgotten but not gone. I had known for a while but could not bring myself to understand as we sometimes do the things we know all along are real and I went from Italy to Memphis, strange route, and I reached the country on a boat loaded with people like yourself of your persuasion religion whatever and they were kind to me telling me that I was pretty as they had always imagined American girls to be and I said Oh, American, am I American? and then understood that that was so although for all these years I imagined myself as something particular to one part of the country only and found the rest of the country as odd and curious and unfamiliar as I found Italy, although when I travelled abroad on that brief trip I was less aware of my surroundings than I had been when I went north or west. They liked to talk about their families they were going to see when the boat docked and asked me where I was going and I told them the truth

I'm going to see my daughter .

How nice, how nice, the women chanted. How nice that you're going to see your daughter. Why, I overheard them talk among themselves, she looks so young, she looks like a little girl herself, her light hair, so pretty, she no wrinkles has at all, a skin of a little girl

Whenever we saw each other on deck they asked are you getting nervous you'll see your daughter soon? So soon how getting nervous she is from the thought of seeing her daughter walking the deck or shivering in my room

It is a far piece from New Orleans to Memphis. And yet I didn't remember the trip up the Old Trace, passing passing red leaves trees fields of such powerful recollections that I might have read all about their attractions before I had even lived it and then lived it and the land seemed to draw all the force and feeling out of me as though itself recognized what I would have to not feel in the day ahead

It was a warm evening towards the end of September when I entered the city for the last time. I had ridden the entire way in a private car a Buick then it was quite the style you know and we drove past the same hotel since I knew that I did not need a bed for the night and even if I did I would not have given my custom to a place such as that with memories of Herbert in the window well in the doorways halls. We rolled past we made the necessary turns I retraced my route quite accurately to the driver and he said

Are you sure you want to go to this place accent on this time he was trying to tell me something he thought I didn't already know and I said

Yes, indeed, that is my destination

And he said,

You're the he hesitated wanted to say boss then substituted lady in charge

Madam you might call me I said

What he said what you sure have a sense of humor ma'am

Do I I said I did once I know I used to dance in vaudeville and play in the moving pictures just bit parts but they required that I have a sense of humor Here we are I said recognizing the house by its door

He pulled the car over to the curb and turned around to face me where I sat without feeling much of the thing in that moment in the rear of the car

Could I know you he said.

IV

The sea gave off the color of blood, as though it were somehow conscious of the plan.

"I don't like the scene tonight," said Bergère, plucking at his tie. "It's too pretty..." He shook his head, suffering privately at the cruelty of their plot and the deep and resonant shades of the water, hills, sky. Veins bulged in his arms, his own blood surging through his brain as though the tide called sooner to him than to the sea. No older than eighteen, his dark eyes showed his lack of sleep and his skin the years he had spent in dimly-lit caverns. I should put my feet up on the bench and smoke a cigarette or two. But instead I'm afraid that I may pee.

"Here they come," said his companion. It was as if they existed each in different spheres until the moment for action arrived. It had been that way before. I am tall, he is short. My bowels. Stubby little fucker who would murder his granny if she tweaked his nose. He dislikes my proletarian origins and I think he smells like the rest of the people of his province whatever their social class. "Time to play magician."

"What's that?" Bergère said, looking up at the couple smiling for the photographer on the beach front. Their black limousine sat at the entrance to the Sandborn-Nice. The man looked quite ordinary in his carefully-pressed blue uniform. The death's head caught the light of the late spring sun. Sprightly walk. Something special there. His teeth would be perfect, and he could do more pushups than anyone in their own unit, of that one could be sure. "... pushup!" Dac's voice broke into his thoughts. He was reading my mind! But no, look at her, she brings out the thought in all men. Her hair nearly the color of the bay, her legs as trim as my baby sister's. And she must be nearly forty!

"... quite a number," Dac finished, speaking through his own clenched teeth as she turned her back to the driver.

"She's American." "She's been with him a year now."

"I don't think I've ever seen an American woman before," said Bergère.

"You must be joking," said Dac as he watched the couple disappear up the hotel steps and through the arches that led into the lobby.

"Why, man, do you think we run a tourist colony up our way? Who wants to swim in our coal mines?"

Dac spat onto the roadway, barely missing Bergère's left shoe. "Well, come on," he said before Bergère could respond to his challenge. "We've got a war to fight. You have your papers?"

"Yes," said Bergère. "But I have to piss something awful."

"Christ, man, at a time like this! What kind of a softie are you?"

"Softie? I've got to piss."

"Okay, okay, do it in the hotel. There's a WC just off the kitchen."

"We have to go up to the second floor anyway. I'll find one on the second floor."

"Maybe you'd like to use the one in their room."

Bergère laughed, in spite of himself. Now he recalled why he enjoyed working with the little florist's son. Both of them lived far from home, both of them made the most of it.

"I'd like to use her," he said, patting Dac on the shoulder as they walked to the path which led to the kitchen's underground entryway. "I wonder what she's like." He touched the knot of his fat red tie.

"We should fuck her," said Dac. "I wouldn't mind that."

"And behave like those animals? I was only joking."

"The war's on. I have no illusions." Dac lowered his voice as they passed the gendarme on duty at the door. "Good afternoon, how you doin'?"

The gendarme raised his eyebrows at Bergère's appearance.

"Who's he?"

"My cousin. He has to pee before he goes to work up the beach."

"He looks tender. Do you have to hold his hand? Or something else?"

Dac showed the gendarme that he thoroughly enjoyed his remark by patting Bergère on the buttocks and shooing him in the door.

"He'll be out in a moment, officer."

"And you too perhaps," the gendarme said, "when they find that you're bringing your entire family in to piss."

"I wish you'd piss on his shoes," Dac said as they climbed the stairwell to the ground floor and then continued on to the second. "There's the little WC at the end of the hall. Do it quickly. We have only a few minutes before the truck leaves the city."

Bergère nodded and walked swiftly down the end of the hall. The room lay in the opposite direction. I could have only a few minutes to live myself, he considered, why do I want to make the time go by so fast? He counted the number of doors he passed, found the water closet and yanked on the door. Locked.

"What?" came a gruff female voice from within.

He did not reply but instead hurried back to where Dac was waiting for him.

"You didn't go in."

"Someone was using it."

"But you still have to piss."

"Don't make me feel like a child. I'll hold out till later."

Dac touched his arm.

"Good, lad. I knew you could do it."

Bergère grew angry, feeling the hard metal piece inside his coat. "No more jokes."

"Jokes keep my mind off things."

"I don't live that way myself."

"You haven't lived that long, kid, that you know how to live. Make the most of it." He talked through his teeth. "And make it short."

"The job, you mean?"

Dac did not have time to reply.

Footsteps behind them. They turned nervously to see a wide-hipped middle-aged woman in a nurse's costume following them down the hall.

"Young man!"

Bergère stopped suddenly while Dac kept on moving a few paces further down the hall.

"Yes, Madame," he said as calmly as he could.

"Was that you outside the door?"

"Come on," Dac said in a voice louder than normal. "Come along."

"Good-bye, Madame."

"I was only trying to inquire — "

"Come on!" Dac insisted, herding his companion down the hall.

Bergère bowed his head, feeling he did not know why quite embarrassed. I am rude to old ladies and I don't know why I'm here. What is this thing in my pocket? What are we doing here? Who are the enemies? What are these questions? How can I walk? Will we make it to the end? My breath, why does it hurt me to breathe? My mother never lived as long as that old bitch but she once worked as a matron at a movie theatre . . .

"Here it is," Dac said, his voice almost sunk to a whisper. "Are you alright? You're trembling."

"My bladder."

"Steady now. Time to play magician."

Dac looked both ways down the hall, then knocked on the door.

The American woman opened it. A voice barked in German behind her, but she moved as though she were walking under water, caressing the door with her right hand even as they forced her back into the dimly-lighted room whose windows lay muffled in thick, purple draperies. The voice barked again from a corner at the bed and they shouted at him and at the woman.

Something in the way she looked at him drew from Bergère a long shiver. Her wide blue eyes, the awareness in that glance, seemed to mate with a wish now revealed to him as she finally released her grip on the door and had they the time he would happily have emptied his aching bladder across the front of her creamy-white silky garment with pearl buttons lying open down the front to show her freckled breasts. Her hands upraised not so much in surprise as recognition, her posture in that instant impossible, fantastic, demanding witness. It would haunt him for the rest of his life.